The Root of the Narrow

David A Craig

© 2010 David A Craig
The Root of the Narrow

ISBN 978-0-9565900-0-8

Published by Ondondy Books
148 Stourbridge Road
Bromsgrove
Worcestershire
B61 0AN

The right of David Alexander Craig to be identified as the author of this work has been asserted by him in accordance with the Copyright, Designs and Patents Act 1988.

All rights reserved. No part of this publication may be produced in any form or by any means – graphic, electronic or mechanical including photocopying, recording, taping or information storage and retrieval systems – without the prior permission, in writing, of the publisher.

A CIP catalogue record of this book
can be obtained from the British Library.

Book designed by Michael Walsh at
THE BETTER BOOK COMPANY

Printed by
Ashford Colour Press
Unit 600 Fareham Reach
Fareham Road
Gosport
Hants PO13 0FW

To Lally who has helped and encouraged so much,
and to Gordon Wood who has always been
ready to make good suggestions

Wo aber Gefahr ist, wächst das Rettende auch"
[But where danger is, redeeming powers grow too"]

1

Birds carve shapes and letters in the clear bright sky. The summer shines. The earth has long breathed out the mist of winter.

"Tell me about that staff hanging there on the wall," Michael asked his father.

The light shone hard onto the dresser above which the staff hung. Michael and his father looked out of the window at the garden that was slowly going dry from the heat. His father shielded his eyes from the glare and then looked again at the wall.

"It was given to us by your great uncle when he moved over here. He had been living beyond the border near the river Ithon, and when he retired he came to live near here, just a little further up the hill."

"Was he very old?"

"As old as I can remember anyone being. The last time he came out we helped him up the hill home, and when we had him back at his place he told us to look in the corner there when we got back. We got back and looked."

Michael looked in the corner where his father had pointed.

"And we saw the staff. It had been lent to him by an old tramp full twenty years before he retired out here. He said there was some charm on it, something or other to make us glad when we needed it."

"How could an old stick like that make us glad? What would anyone want with it? And he never gave it back, did he?"

"No, we took possession of it when he died. I don't think he had ever been asked to hand it back."

"Strange. I wonder what we are supposed to do with it," Michael wondered.

"It's all right hanging up there. It reminds me of my old uncle when I look at it. He was a bit of a character."

The summer was so hot: they sauntered into the kitchen to find ice and a cool drink. Talking was hard. His father took off his tie and loosened the neck of his shirt before he sat down after a hard day.

Michael moved over to the window and looked out westwards, as he judged, over the wide vale to the hills of Wales in the distance. Over these hills the clouds were dropping and their jagged shapes were moving slowly across. After some minutes of vague staring he turned round and came back to the centre of the room, where he stood looking again at the staff. It was a long, perhaps five-foot long, polished staff with odd markings along it. He gazed hard, trying to discern whether it was writing, but he recognized no letters.

"And those markings," he asked," did your uncle Joe do that too? I can't make out if it says anything."

"He restored it. That is to say, he restored what he thought it had once been. He was never certain. He had a man round once, from your school, who claimed to be able to read old writings, but he could make nothing of the script. It's probably an old Welsh shepherd's stick with a motto on it. That's the best guess we can make."

He closed his eyes again and put his feet up on the tuffet. Michael took the staff down from the wall and examined it. He felt it carefully in his hands and ran his palms over the knots of wood. The odd markings were like strange designs to him. They seemed to him to be leaping and jumping along the stick, and with them the energy and enthusiasm of whoever had carved them so long ago, over forty years ago at least.

"So it must be their language – it's in these old signs, and the letters their own. We don't know them in England."

His father was now asleep and Michael feared to disturb him. He went over to the window and looked out at the dropping sun. Still towards the end of July it was there, thumping heat from the sky till quite late. The wild green of the landscape out there excited him. He saw the clouds gathering up into indiscriminate shapes and the hedgerows stretching well beyond the county border over the river to the parts he could explore during the present holidays.

He looked at the changing colours in the sky and the wild riders, the clouds crossing towards north, the evening horsemen, as he called them, always moving northward, winter spring and summer, riding north.

He longed for the chance to walk again over that western landscape, to probe the tracks over the hills as he had done in a mild sort of way when, much younger, he had been guided along them by his uncle Hugh till he had returned home with feet sore from the heat.

He turned round and once more approached the wall where the staff hung. He took it down again cautiously, guiltily almost, so as not to knock anything that might disturb his father in his sleep. He held it inquisitively in his right hand and examined the strange writing and the dried out gnarls, joints as they seemed, of long discarded bones. He clasped the staff at his side and stood to attention while he gazed at himself in the mirror.

"What a fine figure, so upright!" a girl's voice murmured behind him. His sister!

"Admiring yourself again? I'd let someone else do that."

She snatched up a magazine and flung herself indolently into the nearest armchair. Their father half opened his eyes and rebuked her sleepily:

"Do have a heart, Jane, you could have noticed I was asleep."

She settled down to read, mumbling an apology. Michael had already taken the staff out with him through the French windows, down the length of the garden. It glistened and threw the bright evening sun everywhere. He held it aloft, parallel to the line of clouds that streamed across to the north. It seemed to twitch and quiver restlessly in his hands.

"It wants to be back where it belongs," he thought, "out over there somewhere. Some old shepherd cut it down and tokened it."

He waved it at the few sheep which had gathered near the hedge that cut their garden off from the meadow behind. The animals shied away from him, collected in a tiny flock and moved slowly back again.

Michael strolled carefree along the path towards the gate. He felt rested and fresh, full of energy. What he would not give for a walk, a long walk across the valley to the mountains! He stretched his limbs, took a run at the hedge and vaulted over, scattering once again the lazy sheep.

He heard his sister's voice behind him shouting him back, but he did not listen. He was caught by the falling sun's rays and by the charm of this staff, both pulling inexorably towards the west.

Over a field gate leant a farmhand, an old man weary and clearly longing for a night's rest. He beckoned Michael to him, asking:

"That staff, lad, whose is it? Where did it come from?"

His voice sang towards the youth. His face with the sun behind it was indistinct as he called Michael over to him. Michael came over with the staff drooping from his right hand, dragging across the ground. He stopped about five yards from the gate and asked himself who this was. He was certainly not one of the usual farm workers, who by now would be almost too surely in the local over a glass of barley wine.

"My – our staff..." His hand tightened round as he answered.

"Let me see, son," the old man replied. Michael moved towards him, distrustful but curious. He looked up at the strange motions of the birds carving patterns in the air above his head. The sky was darkening, red going to blues and greens. He held out one end of the staff towards the man, that he might examine it while he held it securely at the other end. The man clutched at it eagerly as one clutches at a sword in the scabbard. His old eyes seemed fixed on the inscription. His hands loosed the staff as he looked at the youth.

"This is part of the root, the part that was lost and must be returned."

Michael explained what his father had told him, how great uncle Joe had brought it back, how a tramp had given it to him so long ago.

"Entrusted is given on a lease, my friend," said the old man mysteriously. "Some day the term will expire and it must be given up to the true owners; they will need it when the others come."

"Others? What others?"

The old man continued: "It will not rest much longer where it is, now one of us has seen it again. Look – the birds, the trees all beckon towards it."

And it was true that those birds Michael saw over the man's white head, and trees that swayed in the evening breeze, were showing something like recognition.

2

The beeches were bending in the wind that drifted through their rich foliage. The tinier branches like wings of birds carved designs against the sky and the birds began to settle quietly on the boughs. The old man spoke in the peace of a completed evening.

"These around me are my friends. We are waiting for a return. The deep roots of the world are with us: they are on our side. Give back the staff, son. Give it back when it is asked of you."

Michael turned to go back into the house. He had no desire to be mixed up with this weird fellow, even though his musings somehow fascinated his imaginative side. He walked back towards the little gate into the garden. Then suddenly a thought seized him. He turned round again and asked in a loud voice:

"I suppose you couldn't tell me what this writing means?"

"What is it to tell when the meaning does not come?" The man persisted in talking thus in riddles. "The words, what are they against the blood that spoke them? Know first the blood and then you will know the meaning."

He shuffled off down the path, leaving Michael on his own. The birds were quiet and the trees quite still as now the breeze subsided. Dusk was falling as Michael stepped back into the lounge holding the staff rather awkwardly.

"What on earth have you been doing with that?" was his father's annoyed greeting.

It was not right to remove things from their proper place without consulting. Anyhow, the way Michael was carrying it made his father doubt whether he had really taken care of it. He would be very angry if it were lost or misplaced. It had, after all, a precious history.

"Boys playing at soldiers will commandeer anything," was Jane's contribution. Michael raised the stick to take a swipe at her, but his father took quick possession of it as their mother entered with sandwiches and coffee for the evening. The family sat down and the mother started the conversation: it was sultry and she sensed a storm was brewing.

"The wind's gone and the air is heavy."

"Where are the rain clouds, then?" Jane went to the window and drew back the curtain.

"They're coming. Thick enough to cut out any moonlight."

So it was. The garden, which half an hour ago had been bathed in silver light, was almost swallowed up in the dark. A few drops of rain were falling on the terrace. Thunder, they thought, vaguely in the distance.

"There'll be no storm to match the one when I was a boy. I thought the house had been hit by a shell and spent the rest of the night in Uncle Joe's room clutching his hand. By morning half the garden had been washed away and the glass in the French windows almost blown out of its frame."

As if to defy his remark, the wind had risen again and the rain started to patter steadily on the panes. They all voted to ride out the storm in their beds, if a storm should come. Before he retired Michael glanced once more at the staff. It was swinging almost imperceptibly on the wall. The wind must have got into the room through some crack in the window frame.

He was soon in bed waiting for sleep. He enjoyed this time of day; his mind played with innumerable pictures and events. He lost himself in all that pleased and delighted him: he swam in warm rivers, sailed down luxuriant estuaries, floated high over hills, mountains, waterfalls and tumbling streams, saw stunted trees bent hard by the winds, their foliage like wisps of hair among the grasses and over the rocks. He saw clans of people gathering on the top of some barren hill on the lee-side of an enormous rock. They were shouting, gesticulating, waving anxiously towards a lone figure. Their words seemed loud and frantic, yet Michael heard nothing. He drifted closer to the central figure, tall and majestic against the clouds that rushed behind him in the deep-blue twilit sky. In his right hand he bore an enormous staff. He raised it with an overwhelming cry to those before him. Michael started back in awe. It seemed as if the whole mountain were about to collapse under an imminent crash of soundless thunder. An intense flash of white light lit up his room and disturbed his reverie.

Suddenly the world about him commanded his whole attention; the predicted storm had started; the wind was ripping round the curtains and thunder followed the lightning shaking the glass in the window frame. The rain was washing down outside. Louder and louder the wind rushed through the trees. He got up and went to the window to look out, drawing back the curtain. He saw the wild top branches of the beeches waving their mad designs against the areas of sky where the moonlight still came through.

The second flash was like a giant taking a photograph of the room. Michael leapt back into bed and cowered there as the thunder fell in upon his ears and the wind tore louder round the house. Gradually the intervals between thunder and lightning grew less and less till the thunder almost pounced on the lightning as it whitened all the walls in its extravagance. It was autumn the way the leaves from the weaker trees dashed, loosed from their branches, against the window. The thunder grew louder and louder so that Michael imagined a huge hammer pounding on the roof of the house. He huddled in the bedclothes around him, scared lest the chimneys might fall through or lest part of the structure of the house itself might be struck.

He did not know how long the height of the storm lasted, but at one point, possibly close to the moment it began to subside, he got up, turned on the light and went downstairs, driven by he was not sure what into the lounge, to see the staff once more that night. He trod carefully in his bare feet onto the carpet and switched on the light. There was immediately an enormous flash and the light went out, leaving him in the pitch dark. He looked instinctively towards the window where the meagre light was coming from.

Then all of a sudden the whole extent of the horizon was illuminated by a series of blinding flashes and a wild cool wind shot into the room, enveloped his body and swung round the walls, hoisting the staff nearly off the nail on which it hung. The flashes were succeeded by the tolling of bells of thunder and the scraping sound of the staff, now insecure in its position. Michael played about with the light switch but the light would not go on. The lightning struck back again aggressively at his eyes. He shielded them from the intensity of light. But he was caught by a tapping at the French window, a frantic tapping of someone desperate to be let in. He stared at the window and saw what he made out to be the old man he had encountered that evening in the field, now beckoning wildly to him.

Michael held back: his first reaction was to dash upstairs and to hide himself under the bedclothes. However, an unconscious realization that he was not afraid but strangely inquisitive kept him where he was and slowly drew him towards the window where the figure was still gesticulating. He was within a yard of the window when he caught the words:

"The staff, the staff – now is the time to deliver it! To us boy, reach it out! Deliver the staff! Deliver the staff!"

His hands pounded against the window pleading to be let in. Michael was drawn towards the wall where the object hung and was swinging as if trying to jerk itself free. But he could neither release it and cast it out to the man nor wrench himself away out of the room. He did not understand. He stood rooted there, staring, unable to act. The lightning was flashing intermittently through the glass and gradually the letters on the staff began to glow out, trying, it seemed, to express themselves. Michael saw that the words and their outlines were still unclear and that, as the thunder moved off into the distance, the staff became stiller and stiller and the face at the window had gone.

He was able to move. He went to the door and tried the light. The electricity had been restored. The room seemed normal again. He even dared to tiptoe to the window and look out over the lawn. There was nothing untoward there, just the lone trees dripping rain water and swaying gently in a breeze which was now anything but wild.

3

Michael stalked upstairs in the extreme stillness which follows such storms. He looked from his bedroom window at the glow in the sky, at the gentle approach of day, the new light touching delicately the rippleless pools on the roadway and the softness of the washed colours.

He was surprised at this hour to see a man taking his dog for a walk past the house. The man sauntered down the road apparently gazing inquisitively up at the house as his rough-haired black dog sniffed round the garden. Shortly afterwards the man turned round and walked up the hill. Michael's eyelids fell as he groped his way to bed to fall into a deep sleep.

He took his breakfast much later than the rest of the family, who left off teasing him for his usual late hours as soon as he told them about the storm. He could not believe that they had slept through all that. Only his sister was in any way sceptical.

"Not much of a storm if it only wakes you up," teased Jane, looking at him through her glasses. How severe she could look!

"Quite a storm if it wakes me up, and you've just been on to me about sleeping too deeply."

"You know how deeply Michael usually sleeps," their mother intervened, "and I can see that the storm wrought havoc on parts of the garden. You'd think it close to autumn the way leaves are scattered all over the back lawn."

"And what strange patterns too," Jane added, "like some kind of design ..."

She turned to her brother smiling ironically, "Did you do it yourself? One of your concoctions? If it had been natural you'd have been the last to wake."

Michael was annoyed at the way she never took anything he said without tearing it about and worrying it the way a dog tears and worries a piece of paper.

He told them how the thunder had pounded like a great hammer, how he had gone downstairs and the light had gone out for a time, how he had been scared at what appeared to be a threat to the whole house.

"How selfish of you to leave us all asleep in bed then!" Jane interjected maliciously.

"Thank goodness he did," muttered their father," I don't want my sleep disturbed without good reason."

"All right then, I'm making the whole thing up," said Michael sullenly and he went on eating his toast. He was determined not to tell her anymore. He would be a fool to expect her or even his mother to believe the rest of the events. Perhaps, after all, he had been dreaming – least of all did he want to appear a fool. He took up the newspaper, scanning the pages to see if there were any mention of thunder or storm damage. There was none. But probably the edition was too early to report what had happened in the small hours of the morning.

After breakfast he put on his shoes and went into the garden.

"Careful! Are you sure the thunder's stopped?" Jane yelled after him.

"What's wrong with you? You're all twisted up this morning!" he shouted back at her, and he seemed to have hit on the right words to silence her for the moment.

The state of the garden, though, confirmed his first feelings. It had been ravaged: rain and wind had competed in ruining delicate plants, flattening the sturdier ones and ripping off leaves and the smaller branches of trees. He could see what he imagined to be the remnants of rain and storm clouds lowering over the distant horizon. The sunlight was over there too, in contrast to the overcast sky above him. The light danced and bounced on the gentle hills as it surely must be doing too on the more distant high mountain peaks. There the buzzards rose high over the valleys, carving strange figures in the sky as they waited on their prey. He thought again of his dream and of the staff which they wanted back. Could he believe what he had seen in the middle of the past night? But of course the old man was real; he had been there in the evening when Michael was fully awake.

"Entrusted, given on a lease, and the lease will expire." These words came back from yesterday to occupy his mind. And who were the true owners then? Part of him suggested that he had not really woken up, but another part resented this thought.

"That's your sister's voice plaguing you," his inner voice muttered secretly to him. He tried to repair some of last night's damage. He trod the roots of the plants firmly into the ground and swept as many twigs as he could off the grass. It was as if he himself felt a little responsible for the storm, as if he had had a hand in it.

He was drawn back inside to consult his maps, as he loved doing. To see how the higher hills over to the west were formed – their names, the rivers and hamlets scattered about them, and the courses of numerous streams and brooks which fed the rivers: the lakes too that were eyes reflecting the blue, and the blue looked up to the sky to receive and transmute ever new its images. He traced on the map the paths he had walked with his uncle Hugh, the forests they had roamed in, and the paths and the forests where they said they would some time tread. He wondered where, in the wide expanse, old and dead uncle Joe had found the staff and what it had meant to him.

"Entrusted, entrusted," echoed in his memory. Entrusted for what? Or against what? Perhaps it had been handed over to him as conquered nations had given the British secret documents to preserve from the Germans during the war.

"D'ye want to know where I'm going?" Jane's voice rang out behind him.

"It's hardly on this map," he answered, "and anyway I didn't know you could find your way around maps."

She gave him a sharp kick on the leg. He looked round and scowled at her:

"You want me for something?"

"I'll be glad to be away from you!"

"You're both bored," said their mother intervening, "that's what comes of these long holidays."

"Well, I'd like to go away too," retorted Michael, " though not with her, of course."

"You threw away your chance earlier on," his mother chided him, "and you know we can't all go away together with all the visitors we've had this summer."

"Could I ring Uncle Hugh tonight and see if I could stay with him? That wouldn't cost much."

"You know he's been ill and your father doesn't like troubling him."

"That was some time ago. He'll be better now, and I won't give him any trouble."

"Some hope," Jane whispered.

"Oh, get off to your boyfriends."

That set her into confusion. Her teasing was merely a defence against being teased herself, and Michael was shrewd enough to detect this.

"You can ring your uncle if your father agrees. We'll ask him when he gets home. This evening."

Michael pored again over his maps, enjoying the free rein he was giving his imagination. He spread out the map of their area and sought out an interesting walk he could go on if negotiations with his uncle came to nothing.

At the lunch table their mother told them of the dust everywhere in the lounge that morning, so much had been driven in during the night before the wind had given way to rain. Was Michael sure he had not been daft enough to open the French windows during the storm?

"How on earth could you accuse me of that?" He felt insulted and left the table as soon as they had finished without offering to clear away.

In the lounge the air seemed like fresh mountain air, full of grass, tree and water smells, exciting and wild. The staff was still hanging in its familiar place. He moved towards it to grasp it again, and, as he did so, the song of the birds in the garden seemed to rise up and the colours outside that reached in through the window to his eyes thrilled him again. He took the staff and waved it gently, but in fact it seemed to be waving him. His arm moved, following a strange pattern, a pattern as strange as the letters, carved so carefully on its side.

4

The light, the green soft light that had entered the room seemed to leave again, and as it left it drew him once more to the window. He looked at how the sun was shining down on the garden and on the green and browning fields behind it. The soft, earthy air that follows a thunderstorm had given way to a new fresh, less sultry heat, a heat that provoked energy rather than languor. Michael stretched his limbs as he watched the brighter light filter through the swaying branches.

When his father came home he agreed that Michael should ring his uncle that evening, but he was adamant that he should not go unless he were welcome without conditions. He explained how ill Hugh had been and how hard his life was now, living on his own. He had of course Jack and Kate who helped a great deal, but he still missed his wife, whom he had lost in the war. Michael's mother thought that for this reason alone Hugh might welcome the prospect of Michael's company, even if Michael did go off on his own occasionally.

Just after six o'clock all was settled. His uncle Hugh looked forward very much to having his nephew with him in a couple of days' time. He remembered with pleasure the good times they had had when he was last there. No, Michael would not be any trouble. He could always rely on Kate to pop in and help with the cleaning and meals. If Michael arrived around ten to eleven on the morning train Jack would pick him up at the station. That was settled then. Tomorrow Michael would pack and go down into town to find some agreeable present for his uncle.

The next day passed quickly. Michael was pleased with the bottle of French red wine he had bought as the present. He packed his maps, compass, rucksack, binoculars, walking boots and two books he hoped he would have no occasion to read.

At supper time his father talked about the great knowledge his elder brother had acquired of that area of Radnorshire where he now lived. Michael knew himself how Hugh could hold forth for hours on local legends recent and in the dimmer past. He felt drawn to those stories where history and legend become inseparable and where the colour of romance fixed so hauntingly in his mind. He remembered the Four Stones beneath which the four ancient Celtic kings lay buried, stones marking a resting place on a track that had once been one of royal ways of long-forgotten kings. And there were the strange mounds of stones higher up on the Ridge where the temple of the Grail is said to have stood. And there was far more – paths, tiny clumps of wood, intricate patterns of streams and ditches that criss-crossed that countryside where the greens were lighter and the hedgerows full of mystery.

The night came and he lay in his bed musing, no chance of going to sleep just yet. He lay on his back and stared at the shapes the moonlight gave to the shadows of branches on wall and ceiling. As he lay there his body seemed to become weightless with the staring, as if he were being borne upwards by the sheer power of his concentration. Then he fell back as his heart leapt then missed a beat. Some sort of shock, but what from? His vision had became blurred, but it cleared again; the shadow of a large bird had alighted on the shadow of a branch and was pecking now at the leaves, now at the smaller twigs and, when these had gone, at the branches, at the structure of the tree itself. The bird's wings were knives, cutting sharp shadows into the moonlight on the walls. Then there was only one bird and no tree, just the wings and a beak pecking at the light till the room was in pitch dark.

Michael made for the light and switched it fumblingly on. He dared to look through the window. The tree was still there and the moon light as before – but no bird. In the road the same man as the morning before was there with his dog. But there was no bird.

He threw himself back into bed, covering himself with the sheet and blanket to shut out a recurrence of the nightmare. But the pictures still flashed across his mind as he lay: the picture above all of a tree being eaten by a gigantic shape that grew till the tree was devoured. He was shivering with fright, but still intently turning all those images over in his mind in order to sort them out.

Words flowed through his mind as he thought of the streams and hedgerows of Radnorshire, tracing figures round the copses and larger woods, and of the streams which nature had made and the hedges man had planted mixed inseparably together as his uncle had once told him. They trusted each other, were entrusted like the staff, the staff ... till the lease expired, and it must be delivered back to its owners that it might be used for a new purpose. Otherwise ...

He saw again the image of the great bird devouring the tree and his mind was suddenly seized, or rather guided by an outside force: the staff! Surely it had to be returned: should he take it? He must take it back and find its owners.

Michael was guided downstairs to the lounge where the old staff was hanging. The room was cool and still with the night air. He took hold of the staff, clutched it tightly to him and carried it to his bedroom.

"They'll never notice it's gone till I've left," he thought to himself, "as long as I can go to the station alone."

He felt quickly at ease now and was soon asleep.

He woke with a feeling a great energy and purpose; his stay with his uncle in Radnorshire was to be more than a holiday, it was to be a mission, even a quest, to return this weird staff which, in the last couple of days, had so haunted him. Breakfast passed uneventfully, nobody went into the lounge, nor was there any need to.

"I'll make my own way to the station," said Michael as he had checked that he had the money for the fares and his building society savings book. His mother had packed the wine for his uncle and besought him to write a card or two to keep in touch. Jane remained quiet, looking vaguely at the newspaper. Michael thought she envied him. True, she was going away later, and he was sure she did not one hundred per cent relish the forthcoming camping holiday further west near Rhayader. No boys at a girl guide camp!

He put on his raincoat with the excuse that clouds were gathering, in order to hide the staff beneath it. He said goodbye and set off on the road carrying his case to the bus stop. On the way he passed that man with the dog. The man's eyes followed him inquisitively while the dog strained at the leash to sniff.

In a quarter of an hour Michael was in the train to Craven Arms where he changed for the train into Wales. The two-coach train travelled along the single line past Bucknell to Knighton. He felt the hardness and the uncanny warmth of the staff against him as the landscape changed and became more hilly. He removed his coat for some relief from the warmth of the day. Soon he was at his destination. Across the railway line on the opposite platform he thought he recognized the old man standing there. He heard his name called, and there was Jack waiting for him with the car.

How glad he was to see Michael again and how much his uncle was looking forward to seeing him! He started, and they set off to his uncle's house just a couple of miles out of Presteigne. Michael glanced around him. Surely there was that old man again on the other side of the road, fixing him with knowing eyes. Michael clutched at the staff and took in the wide lofty landscape that was now coming into view.

5

The gently undulating plain of the West of England had given way and was opening out into the grander hills of Radnorshire, to the fields with sudden dips in them, tumbling down to hidden brooks and wild bunches of trees shielded thus from the wind, to hills smoothed on their tops by wind and rain, but with sudden unexpected cracks where the rocks pushed out and waterfalls tumbled. To stand aloft on those hills and look out westwards gave one a sense of awe at a landscape growing wilder and wilder, spreading out farther and farther to the most distant skylines.

Michael knew this; he had stood there times before with his uncle and gazed out to the west on clear days, when the rains had washed through the sky and the thin streaks of clouds tinged with the light-blue of a fresh sky afforded a view of enticing dimensions. What a thrill it was to be carried back here again, to be in it and walk across it, and grasp it in his hands in an attempt to become part of it!

He shook his head in an instinctive attempt to try to arrange in some order the variety of dreams that had visited him asleep and waking in these past days. Still he held the staff and felt with his little finger the incision of the inscription on it. It seemed to have its own weird supply of electricity that shot into his limbs, making them ache with the energy that said: move! move!

He felt with his hand the texture of the staff as his eyes searched the landscape, seeking out an area whither he might possibly go in his desire to give it back to whomsoever it might belong. But he was too dazzled by the vastness before him for his eyes to fasten on any one place which instinct or inspiration might prompt him to recognize as the place to which the object should be returned. The black crows flying above him in their hasty pattern amid the soft lines of the trees took his mind back to that threatening outline of the great bird's head. The tree, down to the trunk itself, had been absorbed into that enormous maw. Had nothing remained which might take root again?

"Did you see that old chap in the town? I think he's followed me here."

"Him?" answered Jack. "He's been around since long back, Old Owen. No need to take notice of him."

"He looks very much like the old farm fellow who works in the field behind our house. I'm sure he's followed me here."

"Well, Michael, I know Old Owen when I see him. You'll be mixing him up, no doubt. Anyway, he's no harm to anyone, though there're folks around here who say he's not quite right."

Michael was back in himself again, trying to connect the old man with those other things that had been passing through his mind. At the same time his eyes stared, struck over the land that was receiving him. The car suddenly lurched over a large stone in the road, jolting him from his reverie.

"Watch yourself! Hold tight! We want to get you to your uncle in one piece."

"All right, I'm OK."

Michael looked around to ascertain where they were. They had just turned onto a more main road. Not much further to go now, he judged. He remembered from his last visit how here the greens became softer in the fields and hedges and trees – and they took a sharp right-hand turn down a lane, and some hundred yards further on right again up the drive to his uncle's house. There it stood in front of him – firm in the earth, secure, yet by no means asleep, with a welcoming open door and the tall beeches and birches on all sides bent away from the prevailing wind.

The crunching of the car wheels on the gravel as it drew to a halt outside the house brought Kate dashing out, apron flapping. She welcomed Michael heartily, shaking his hand and inquiring about his family, as she and Jack both helped him down with his luggage. They left it for the time being in the cottage porch, intending to shift it over to the big house later after Michael had eaten.

Michael sat at their old, plain oak kitchen table, waiting for the meal they were to serve him, looking all around him as the atmosphere of the area set itself deeper and deeper in him. Most of all he recalled the smell – the dark, rich, musty smell of the houses in these parts.

His uncle lived alone in the big house a short distance behind the cottage. Jack and Kate had their own small-holding which they ran as well as looking after Uncle Hugh's two or three acres. Since he had retired some years ago, this arrangement had been just what Jack wanted. Michael could remember the harder times before Jack's retirement, when he had to be up and away so early, on his bike down the lane to attend to the wishes of Colonel Duggan. Uncle Hugh had moved here with his wife Aunt Alice just before the war, when he and Alice had left the house in the charge of Jack and Kate. Hugh had been sent off to the Far East – Burma and Siam, while his wife had worked in London. It was there in 1940 that she had met her death in the Blitz, and after the war Hugh had returned here to try to live out his life alone. It had been hard, as Michael had been told by his father; he had frequently been out here on a visit when Michael was very young. His uncle had often come to stay with them for quite long periods, especially in those hard winters immediately following the war. But most of all, Michael saw his uncle Hugh and his house as a home where one spent exciting holidays.

Kate explained that his uncle was at the moment not at the peak of health:

"He has been working too hard inside, in that tiny room of his," she told him. Sometimes he had been working late into the night. She had seen his light burning some nights when he had been restless. That must have been at three or four in the morning. And only that winter he had been taken ill again, overdoing it, she added. Nevertheless, Michael rushed through his meal, anxious to see his uncle again and to see with his own eyes the state of the house and its sole occupant. He did not have to wait long; with a knock at the door and a shout, his uncle was in the parlour and shaking his hand, deluging him with questions about his family and the school and other things Michael would rather have forgotten. They both bade goodbye for the moment to the old couple and strode in through the blue-painted front door of the big house. Hugh led Michael upstairs to the room he usually had when he stayed and placed his luggage on the bed.

"What's this?" his uncle's eyes were riveted on the staff, as it lay huddled in Michael's raincoat. He picked it up and examined it thoroughly.

"Do you know anything about it, how Uncle Joe got it and what he was supposed to do with it?" Michael asked.

"I know Uncle Joe left it with your father in the month he died. He said it had meaning for some folk out here, and that he had been entrusted with it till they asked for its return. But he's been dead for many years, and still no one has asked for it back as far as I know."

Michael said nothing of his recent experience but just asked him about the strange lettering.

"Well, it could be Welsh or a kindred Cymric tongue, I suppose. But what a weird gnarled old bit of wood. It might have come from a witch's broomstick. It certainly looks as if it could cast spells."

It was not clear whether he was joking.

"What does Cymric mean?"

"Cymric? A word for the ancient Britons and their name for themselves. It means brothers or something similar. Perhaps they felt they were a brotherhood when the tribes from the east threatened them. A sort of solidarity. Maybe they had an ancient secret that would keep them together and remain effective only so long as they did so together – the Welsh are all that remains of these people, and they're in danger of losing their identity with the English pressing so hard on them. If their old language goes so will so much else, their secrets too."

Michael smiled happily; his uncle had kindled his imagination again, as he always did, when he got talking. This was exactly how he hoped his holiday here would begin.

"As for the strangeness of this staff," his uncle continued, fingering it between thumb and index finger, as if he did not wish to grasp it too tightly, "I simply feel it has some mystery to it. It has an uncanny effect on me, that's all."

"Who knows," Michael contributed. "Something may happen to stop the old language disappearing."

"You like to see the positive side. But back to your query: I don't follow this lettering at all."

He looked at it carefully again. Michael watched the tall gaunt man, with his furrowed face that showed kindness as well as worry. His hands were large but gentle, and his blue deep-set eyes were warm.

His uncle left him to unpack, indicating that he had work to do, and saying that they should meet in the cool of the evening for dinner in the library. Michael knew he had a free run of the house and gardens, and knew too where things were, should he need anything.

6

The breezes that blew against the upper windows of the house were gentle, intermittent, punctuated every now and then by a sudden strong gust. At this moment, it was sounds which first pulled Michael's attention – the bleating of sheep on the hillsides, the brushing of branches on the window pane – no regular musical rhythm – and the low creak of the floorboards as he moved to and fro unpacking, sorting things out quickly into drawers and cupboards as he saw fit.

He found the map of the area and threw himself onto the bed to peruse it at leisure, to plan where he should go and what he should look for. He took his field glasses and looked out onto the land before him, returning frequently from the window to the map to ascertain what each landmark was. He was fortunate that his eyesight was better than his sister's, and that he needed to wear no glasses to see the landscape clearly. He was determined to plan things thoroughly this time. He was, most of all, looking forward to a long expedition lasting a whole day. Out onto the far horizon hills he trained his binoculars, noting the different and all magical shades of green, of meadow, hedge, tree and hilltop near and far. Seldom did his eyes alight on a man or woman out there. Perhaps in a field, down a lane he might see someone urging on a flock of sheep, but he did not long hold this in mind. By now the layout of the land itself was become clear to him. Behind the hills over there was Bach Hill, and beyond was a valley or a plain, where the Four Stones stood, and beyond that the quarry masking Hanter Hill and Hergest Ridge. The Ridge was that twilight borderland between England and Wales. He would need a bike to get that far: perhaps Jack would take him there.

The rest of the day he spent looking at the animals and wandering around the tiny estate. He chatted with Jack and helped him with the horses. He wished he could ride competently; no use learning now, of course, for the time taken up learning would deny him time for exploring. Perhaps he would learn when he was at home again, providing he could find a stable where there were men learning as well as the usual bunch of girls.

He felt so free and entirely happy as he lay on the lawn writing a quick letter home to tell of his safe arrival and send "love and regards" from all here. He confessed having taken the staff with him and hoped they'd understand. The trees over him swayed their gentle branches and the fully fleshed leaves filtered some of the light that fell on the paper. He sealed the envelope and looked back up at the tall trees. All was so still that, without straining, he heard the rustle of the topmost branches as he raised his head. There too were the familiar patterns of bird and tree traced against the sky, though here these patterns were somehow more akin to the movements on the ground and seemed imbued with more life. He was frustrated that he was so near to all this and yet shut out as a child is shut out from adult conversation. He was separated and wanted to become a part.

The sky was a heraldic blue. One wished for a lake large enough to reflect all of it.

Kate had started to prepare the dinner and Michael went up to his uncle's library to browse through the books. As a child he had thought this the most boring room in the house, but now, it was the place where roots are struck and acquaintance made with the occupants of the building. This evening he was drawn to the wide selection of maps and travel books; he became absorbed in the photographs of the East, especially in one huge volume printed in Bombay. The book drew him to maps, and the maps back to books again, and encyclopaedias, till quite an array of books lay spread out on the floor.

The gong sounded for dinner and he was late down, so long did it take him to put everything back. A pity really that that was necessary, as he would surely return there after dinner, if he could.

"Real Cymric lamb," said Michael, smiling as his uncle carved the joint.

"Not from these hills, though," was the reply. Most of the lamb came from Caernarvonshire. They were very Welsh over there.

After dinner his uncle excused himself again, leaving Michael to himself till bedtime. He returned to the library immediately to find out more about the East.

Once in the library, he flitted from one book to the next, unable to settle on one, till he at last realized he had spent the last hour poised over a huge outspread map of the area in which he was now residing. A pang of annoyance shot through him as he became aware that he had forgotten to ask about a bike. But, he supposed, the morning would do, and he did not plan his excursion to Hergest Ridge till Sunday at the earliest. He wanted to explore the immediate neighbourhood first, this side of the Radnor Forest.

He folded up the map and pulled out a book of horror stories. Just the right sort of thing to read before going to bed, surely! Which one then? *Terrors of the Jackdaw*, *Returned from the Grave* ... Finally he settled on *The Wolf of the Harz Mountains* by Frederick Marryat. He read rapidly through the pages as the wild, black, forested humps of the ancient Harz mountains rose before his eyes, the axe and the heavy tread of the forester rang in his ears, and the wild animals and strange lights of the region all rose to occupy the room of his mind:

".... 'What danger there can be to you, which I am not equally exposed to, I cannot conceive,' replied Philip: 'however –' Hardly had he said these words when there was a tremendous roar like a mighty wind through the air – a blow which threw him on his back – a loud cry – and a contention. Philip recovered himself, and perceived the naked form of Krantz carried off with the speed of an arrow by an enormous wolf through the thicket ..."

Michael was holding the page close to his eyes as the shadows in the room lengthened. A cold jet of air ran down his back as he read the final paragraph. He leapt up, switched on the light, amazed that he could have read so much in such darkness. The end of the story reverberated in his mind as he saw the body of the unfortunate Krantz dragged away to be violated in the bushes. The tale hinted at a cooperation between the beasts in the animal world, a cooperation that assured vengeance and a paying off of debts.

He placed the books and the maps back on the shelf and made sure everything in the room was in order. Outside the evening singing of the birds was drawing to a close as night veiled the house, cutting the eyes within off from the wide expanses without. He heard Jack moving in the yard below, locking up the garages and the sheds. A light from a cottage far out over the hills came on. The soft night wind stirred in the trees and cast shadows, thrown by the light from Jack and Kate's cottage onto one of the darker walls of the room. The shadow made a pattern, but Michael could not, even with his often overactive imagination, decide what it might be.

Outside a dog was barking; at first off and on, then steadily its noise grew in an inexorable crescendo. It was scratching at something, a door perhaps?

Michael heard the front door knocked open and the sound of animal feet rushing upstairs. The barking had stopped but there was a fanatical scratching at one of the doors. Michael hurried out of the room when he heard his uncle shouting:

"What on earth is that? See what it is Michael!"

Michael rushed round the landing till he came to his room. An enormous black dog was savaging the door, trying to scratch it open or break in through a weak panel.

"Get it out of here!"

His uncle was behind him, shrieking in his ear:

"Get out!"

They both rushed at the dog which bared its teeth, snarled, then slunk off fast downstairs and out into the lane. His uncle made fast the front door and commented on the damage the dog had done to the door of Michael's bedroom. He wondered what on earth had possessed it to rush in like that.

He wished Michael a good night and returned to his room. Michael entered his, wondering what the animal could have scented. He washed and changed into his pyjamas. An owl was hooting from a clump of trees just the other side of the lane. Michael looked round for something to read before he put the light out. He found his own map which lay on top of the staff on the chair by the door.

7

The water that sometimes trickled, sometimes rushed down the bed of the brook on the far side of the road was almost inaudible during the day, but at night-time the soft, liquid rhythm infected the air with vigour sufficient to stir the stranger from shallow sleep into vague reveries that would lead his mind from the running waters to the rustle of the trees, the creaking of old boughs and the lonely cry and hooting of the birds of night. Michael's fantasy was captured thus and strayed from sound to sound in the restfulness of the night, till all sounds acted as background to the howling in the far distance, maybe a disconsolate dog on some isolated farmstead.

His attention fixed for a while on the old oak door of his room, the crack in it where the light from the landing filtered through. His uncle must still be up working, a safeguard at least against that dog, that dog which had scratched at the door, trying to force its way through it. It was after the staff; Michael was sure about it now – yes, the staff, which had somehow worked on his will to make him bring it back here nearer to where it belonged.

Well, what of this dog then? Had it been sent to retrieve it? Should Michael hand it over? But to whom and where? Should he let the beast take it whithersoever it willed? The sound of trees, hedgerow, brook and wind that touched them all, becoming one sound, took up his thoughts once more, confused them, led them off in fantasies. Could he focus his thoughts and get rid of all this confusion?

"Given up to the true owners....." the words of the old man... "Given up..." – not taken back, Michael was sure he recalled those words accurately. Those whose staff it was would reclaim it, and he would willingly deliver it up to them;

he would not let it be taken or stolen. And the dog? A thief surely, sent by enemy forces, other forces, not the emissary of the rightful owners – they would surely show themselves and claim it. Till that time came Michael must guard it, take care of it.

Tired and almost falling asleep as he stood up, he took the staff close to him and fell asleep in bed with it at his side.

* * * * *

And it was to the incessant trickling of the water of the brook outside that he awoke to feel around him the fresh, sweet air of Radnorshire, air that had the soft scent of wild fern and the rough feel of heather. With enthusiasm for his first day here, he pushed back the musings which had occupied his mind of the night before, shot into the bathroom and his clothes, devoured a breakfast of home-cured bacon and rich-yolked eggs and pored over the map, deciding where he would begin his explorations this sunny morning.

"I'll make you a lunch-packet that will last till this evening and then you can go out and leave your uncle in peace. He doesn't like being disturbed when he's doing all this work," remarked Kate as she cleared away the uneaten toast. "Here," she pointed to a rucksack on a chair, "is all you'll need."

Michael had decided after all against taking a bike and instead to walk on the public footpaths across country to Bach Hill and to make further plans there when he could see the lie of the land better. The hill was over one thousand feet high and must afford a good view all round.

He was about to set off when he came across his uncle strolling idly round the garden, pulling off faded blooms and uprooting large weeds. He was obviously taking a short break from his work. He greeted Michael with a smile, hoping he had slept well following the strange incident of the dog. That, he assured his nephew, was a unique event in the household.

"Perhaps you're the first person here with an attracting scent," he grinned.

Michael returned the grin, partially blinded by the reflected light from the greenhouse glass. He saw a somewhat distorted outline of the figure of his uncle, carrying in one hand a weed dripping with soil and in the other a few flowers which Michael feared his uncle might crush without realizing it. But the kind weather-beaten face, as he drew away from the reflected light, told him that he feared needlessly. Hugh had gathered these flowers to brighten up his study. He placed them in a vase delicately as if he had scarcely touched them and, at the same time, expressed courteous regret that he had no time today to accompany Michael, although he looked forward to hearing all about his day when his nephew returned in the evening.

Michael hastened to leave the premises now that he had seen his uncle. He gathered his supplies for the day and set off over Court Farm land, crossed the lane and struggled up the hill towards what the map showed as Ednol Farm, clasping the staff firmly in his right hand. Perhaps he might find here a secluded place where he could read, should the day prove hot enough to rule out much energetic activity. He sat down a little out of breath to consult the map. He seemed more or less on the right track, though he wished he had brought his compass with him. Just above him, past Ednol Farm, he should find the remains of an ancient church.

What he thought must be the ruins he found immediately before the forest plantation. He sat down again; it had become so hot that a thin heat haze was hovering over the parts of the landscape he had left behind him, obscuring the horizon. He sat on an upturned boulder that must have formed part of the church. The land below was quite still in the approaching midday heat. He gazed down on it, not exactly conscious of the impression it made on him. These impressions, nevertheless, seemed to go deep; they bypassed words which, if he had tried to express how he felt, would have come up with untruths, as light seen from the shade lies about itself. The awareness that he was unable to articulate his feelings frustrated him and surrendered the energy that would have gone into words to his hands and the rest of his body. He felt a strong desire to lie and roll like an animal on the earth around and under him.

He tried to trace the outline of the ancient church. Certainly the outlines were so vague that he would have missed them had the map not told him. It had been a building of some sort, yes, but if a church, where could the tower have been, or had there been a tower? He looked for a pattern that might explain the layout, but found nothing. All had been erased, long ago. Perhaps the cartographers had made a mistake.

He looked at the dusty soil at his feet. Somebody had been here not long before him, had probably sat on the same boulder and drawn or doodled in the soil, although he could make nothing of the shapes there. The hand that held the staff was itching and felt a strange thrust within itself, maybe almost guiding him to trace those designs in the soil. He did so before he realized he had done it, and immediately afterwards had the urge to stand up and move forward up the hill. The sun was shining straight into his eyes and was blurring his view of how he was to climb higher. But he pulled on upwards.

The hill, rounded by millennia of rains and wind, with its embedded rocks and outworn paths, had surely been crossed by wanderers and even knights of old on missions long forgotten. If only he knew the words, he imagined he would find himself back in their days amongst them and knowing their tasks. But once again words let him down, and he remained on the brink, blurred by the sun and distracted by trivial thoughts from that world he fancied he would like for a moment to enter and be part of. This landscape seemed to live in its past and show itself on a slender lease to the present.

Once more he contemplated the weird signs on the staff and felt that it too was dragging itself with him to those days where it had its origin and essence. It had become like an extension to his body, which he needed to lead him on.

He found his way through the relatively newly planted forest towards the summit of the hill. The staff helped him to beat a path through the nettles and the shade provided coolness at the hottest time of the day. The light green of the larches filtered the strong sunlight, and the damp needles underfoot from last autumn softened the ground to his tread. It was like a picture in a book of fairytales. Michael worked his way over the half-rotten fallen branches and stumps of trees that had started to push out but had been cut off in growth. The coolness here gave him renewed energy, and soon he had quickened his pace and reached the other side of the forest. Before him stretched countless clumps of whortleberries. Despite the violence of the now direct rays of the sun, he sat down and began to pluck avidly the berries from the inviting bushes. Then he continued his climb, enjoying the moist fruit in his mouth.

He was on the summit. He stood erect like a proud king with his sceptre, surveying the realm beneath. It was a land of wonder. He could only respond to it through the energy the sight of it shot into his limbs, tugging at him to explore its wealth. He flopped to the ground and spread the map out before him on the coarse grass, laying the staff across it lest any breeze on the summit blow it away. He looked with the fieldglasses across the valley south east towards Hanter Hill and Hergest Ridge. Over all he observed the black birds carving in wild geometry the midday sky. The undiscovered alphabet of their flight seemed to speak out from the very earth of this land. He raised the staff to trace out nearer to his eyes some of these patterns, and he found he was tracing outlines of stones, megaliths for ancient churchyards, mounds for bygone rulers and their retinues. Still the birds hovered.

He was on the point of descending the hill towards the various standing stones he had located in the distance, when a large black dog came bounding aggressively towards him, half barking, half growling. That dog again, certainly, that had broken into the house, that had haunted him so in his dreams last night. He waved the staff at it to ward it off, and immediately the animal yelped, turned tail and fled down the hill into the forest. Michael too was frightened. He wanted to leave this spot at once. He picked up his things and started scrambling down the hill without looking for a path. He tripped over whortleberry bushes until he reached the lower ground where the going was easier. Behind him he heard a wild barking, sounding half in fear, half in anger – followed by a howling that was dimmed by the larches. Before him was the road and new territory.

8

He scarcely dared turn to see if the dog were following. He glanced round once and thought he saw a black shape leaping up above the height of the larch trees, up there on the slope. And at that moment the air seemed full of barking and yelping that shook through him. Yet these sounds were not within him but above him on the hill, haunting, menacing him as he strode out and ran towards the hedges and farmland of Kinnerton. Surely he was imagining all this; he had heard of people who saw and heard things that seemed real but were merely figments of an overactive imagination. All the same he grasped the staff tightly and tried to feel confident, aware all the time that without this stout stick as companion he would be alone amongst these fears.

He took breath behind a hedge, spreading out his map on the grass of a meadow. There were standing stones close to Kinnerton, and some either side of the lane which led down to Walton. These last stones stood more or less halfway between the top of Bach Hill and Old Radnor church, he worked out.

The ancient look of Kinnerton took his mind off his fears: the old rugged church tower and the leaning gnarled houses worked on his fantasy, pulling him back into time past. He ate a few sandwiches, packed everything again but for the map, grasped the staff and set off through the village to find the nearest standing stones.

He crossed over the rough ditch-track to New Radnor and suddenly there they were on his right, rearing above the height of the hedge, standing on an isolated grass patch in the middle of a ploughed field. The massive blocks were like monstrous bones emerging from the flesh of the grass and were reflecting the powerful rays of the summer sun from their weather-polished surfaces. They dazzled so, that, for a moment, Michael was blinded by the light, seeing nothing but stars and a red streaky glowing. He wiped his brow, shielded his eyes and ran to the gate. In a trice he was over it and beside the stones, as on a platform raised above the general level of the field. He leapt onto the tallest stone and sat upon it. He was on the shoulders of a giant! Then bump! He had slipped off and landed smartly on his backside beside the staff and his pack.

He sat half dazed, surprised at his sudden fall, gazing absently around him; the hills, the hedgerows and scattered cottages were for a moment blurred, like what he imagined his sister must see without her glasses, and in that blurred moment he felt a rumbling underneath him that seemed to vibrate upwards to the area of grass where the stones stood, as if they were the natural outlet for this subterranean noise; strangely connected it all was with these stones, for now they were reflecting, with increasing power, the intense gathered sunlight. He was partially blinded which upset his other senses: he could not make out whether the stones had moved or not. Yet surely the earth under him was stirring. He grasped the staff tighter and tighter, till it seemed that his knuckles would soon pierce through his flesh, and the staff form an intercellular union with his hands. He could not, definitely not at that moment, have shaken himself free. He would have been fixed there, maybe for years, with these stones rearing upwards like growing pyramids around him, taking him into their world.

Then, just as quickly, all had passed and he was seeing clearly again. He sat amongst the stones surveying the marvellous landscape that stretched up and beyond on all four sides, promising so much, so open to his eyes – yes, to all his senses, for he could smell the soft blossomed air and hear the song of many birds. The stones now were as his guardians, protecting him from unseen onslaught and at the same time urging him out further afield to explore and record. What a moment ago had been to him solid mists swirling up from underground waters, were now still in outline and steady in pattern, pointing out to the land around him.

He took hold of the map again, consulted it briefly and after some measurement decided he had time to walk up to Old Radnor church. Thus from the shade of these monoliths he set off south-eastwards down the lane to the main road, along that for a hundred yards or so, then up left to the church with its ancient Celtic cross.

He was at the tumbledown lychgate into the churchyard, entered the porch and pushed open the hefty oak door and went inside. He stood quietly in the nave and looked around the silent building. He was attracted by the old stone font, worn like the knuckle of a giant – a stone moreover like those he had just left in the bed of the valley.

He was determined to ask his uncle about the standing stones to ask whether there might be a connection between that in the church and those below. He was muttering to himself, theorizing extravagantly as to their origin and history, sifting one idea then another till he had quite a shock to hear his own voice echoing round the dry and empty building.

Talking to himself again, the first sign of madness – that was what his sister would say – how she taunted and irritated him whenever he found something of absorbing interest, feigning, as he was sure she did, a 'couldn't care less' attitude in an attempt to dampen or trivialize his enthusiasm. If this were madness he liked it; it made life exciting and vital to him. Who was it who had said, one needed a little madness to keep oneself sane? Never mind. He would keep his enthusiasm, even though there was no one to share it with him and he would continue to talk to himself when moved to do so.

He walked back along the narrow lane through Evenjobb and Beggar's Bush. The sun was still hot, and he stopped whenever he crossed running water to sip from the brook.

The countryside in August was beginning to look tired and worn through the constant sun and the warmth of a season that demanded so much energy from the soil. The greens were fading from their June intensity in exposed places. Under the broad leaves the birds perched silently, save every now and then a small flock rose up black against the deep blue sky. They had been disturbed by some stranger or by the whim of a cooling wind in the later afternoon.

By the time Michael reached his uncle's his throat was parched and he drank what must have been pints of orangeade kindly supplied by Kate. She had already begun to prepare the evening meal, a large meat and salad dish.

On inquiring where his uncle was Michael was told he was still working hard and should not be disturbed yet. He would come down when he was ready. It was dangerous to disturb a man working as concentratedly as he was. What then, Michael wished to know, was he working at? Kate thought a diary perhaps, or some account of his married life. Michael had never known Aunt Alice, a fine person, kind and thoughtful with a good sense of humour, someone to whom Jack and Kate would always be grateful.

Diaries, thought Michael, and his mind flitted uneasily over the times he had teased Jane his sister about her diaries and the secrets he guessed she was hiding in them. He sat down to read till his dinner came.

He was disappointed then too. He had hoped for some conversation with his uncle, but he was disinclined to enter upon anything beyond the usual courtesies and routine. He sat twiddling bits of bread between his large fingers, staring in front of him. Michael was afraid to disturb his thoughts.

"I saw that dog again, but it ran away when I took my staff to it," he ventured, but his uncle did not seem interested. They sat for half an hour together saying nothing, till his uncle muttered:

"We might go to Presteigne market the day after tomorrow."

Michael helped Jack for a time with the horses, especially with one old horse that was sick. He sat down intending to read, but felt as sleepy as in a boring French lesson at school. He dragged himself to bed and fell asleep, quite unconscious that night of the workings of nature outside his window.

9

The next day there was no sun; the air was thick and heavy and lay heavy on Michael's shoulders.

"There'll be thunder," his uncle remarked at breakfast "Let's hope it comes and goes quickly."

Michael looked out of the window at the monotonous shades of grey that occupied the sky and watched as the rain fell onto the flagstones outside the drawing room, creating its own pattern only to obliterate it almost immediately.

Clearly it was not the right day for a further expedition. He had no desire to be caught up in torrential rain and violent storms. These he would rather leave to his imagination or observe from the confines of the house. He therefore decided to remain in the vicinity today.

Very soon he was interrupted in his inspection of the library by the arrival of the vet, who had been called out to look at the sick horse. He jumped up at the loud knocking at the door and followed the vet at a distance as he went over to the stables where Jack was waiting for him. The horse was nervous and started to kick out. It was some time before the vet was able to examine it thoroughly. It's this weather today, Michael thought. He was tense and irritable himself, longing to get out but contained and kept indoors by the present skies and the threat of worse.

"Keep him warmer in the evening especially as the autumn comes on, and give him a drop of brandy now and again, just to loosen his limbs."

The vet gave Jack a small bottle of pills and continued to ask all sorts of questions till Michael became bored with the constant drone and drifted out onto the lane.

But the sky was overcast and heavier rain threatened. He could see nothing of the hills. They were merely a blur to his eyes and hard to distinguish from low cloud. The birds, yesterday so apparent in the sky and around the house had disappeared. He too disappeared into the house in order to write home. He had received a letter this morning, he felt rather too soon, asking how his uncle was and how he had settled in, so Michael decided to send a quick answer off before he pushed it to the back of his mind. His father was evidently concerned about the health of his elder brother, and Michael in his hastily scrawled letter attempted to reassure him that he had nothing to worry about. Uncle Hugh was well, perhaps just a little tired, but he had after all been working late into the night in the short time Michael had been here. Michael told those at home of his plans and of the promised trip with his uncle into Presteigne, when he hoped to have more chance to talk with his uncle. He did not mention anything about his sister's camping holiday in the hope that she would not take it into her head to come down here from Rhayader and interrupt his stay, although secretly he wished she could somehow see what a good time he was having here without her.

He sealed, stamped and addressed the envelope, put on his anorak and set off down the lane to post it. No one else was out except for a girl of about his age whom he passed. She smiled faintly as she went on her way. On his way back the downpour began. It was as if a dam had burst in the sky, and on the horizon wild flashes of lightning lit up the landscape for a split second. All animals and birds had vanished from sight. Only the hedgerows and trees seemed to endure these torrents. His anorak was soon soaked through. The wild flashes continued to light up the land like a mad extravagant photographer. The thunder that followed shook the earth. Suddenly one flash illuminated the hillside to his left, and Michael glimpsed the single gaunt figure of a man, his arms outstretched, standing on what must have been a huge stone or high bank. He seemed to be reaching up to the sky. It was a man pleading, summoning, calling some force to himself as though his life depended on it – or so it appeared to Michael's vivid imagination. Then he saw nothing save the soaked green around him. He ran back to the house to change into dry clothes.

Running made him wetter than ever. He had to take a hot bath and have a complete change of clothes before he felt at ease again. Kate thrust a cup of tea into his hand and directed him to take another to his uncle. Michael was glad of a reason to join Uncle Hugh and find out what he was doing in his study. He knocked timidly at the door and was ordered in.

"Ah, thank you, Michael. I heard the bathwater running. You had a bath then?"

"Did I disturb you? I got soaked and Kate told me to take one."

"It doesn't matter. I couldn't concentrate. Sit down and tell me what you've been doing."

Michael related the proceedings of this uneventful day.

"I saw no one when I was out, except a girl walking down the lane."

"Oh, she's the daughter of a librarian who lives near by."

But Michael wanted to get back to what his uncle was doing.

"Are you writing a book, Uncle?" he inquired nervously. He had been told so often not to be nosy, yet how else was he to find out anything worth knowing unless he was inquisitive? He naturally wanted to satisfy his curiosity.

"Well, a sort of book, if I can get properly down to it. That is, it's a sort of diary of events of the years with your aunt before she was killed."

He looked Michael straight in the eyes as he said this.

"Oh don't worry," he assured him, "I can talk about it. Everybody lost someone in the war. Time does heal although there is a scar. At times I am lonely and wish her here with me and this, I suppose is the way I can bring her back. That's all. I am of course sorry that she went before we had children."

"Perhaps your book can be your child. I read that somewhere."

"What, that men create works of art and women children?"

"Yes, don't you believe it?"

"No I don't. What about Jane Austen? She is one of our greatest writers."

His uncle paused smiling, as if he was thinking of all sorts of things which Michael did not understand or had never come across. Hugh Pritchard took another sip of tea and continued:

"If I did write something that was published, a book that is about us, it would, as you say, be a sort of child – or better, an offspring, but far removed from a real child. A child is not just an offspring: it reacts back at you and you react back at it. A book must be far more rigid, although I suspect that authors of good novels let their characters develop and do not contrive to manipulate them."

Michael thought he understood most of what was said; books were always what they were, but Heaven only knew what his sister would be from one day to the next.

Uncle Hugh sat musing aloud in his chair about the evenings he and Alice used to spend together at the fireside in their drawing room. She played the piano while he read or studied papers he had brought home. Then his uncle jumped up and summoned Michael to follow him into the garden. The rain had stopped and they were enjoying walking together. Gazing at the flowers rich in dripping moisture.

"Just a bit of heat tomorrow after this rain and the garden will forge ahead," his uncle remarked.

Then he turned to talk of that wild dog that had got into the house the other evening. They would have to keep the doors securely shut. Stray dogs such as that one were a nuisance, and he could not see that one lasting long once a farmer had it in his sights.

"Well. Tomorrow you'll come into Presteigne with me?"

Michael affirmed that he would like to and looked forward to the trip.

10

The soft words of this conversation still rang in his mind as Michael awoke and lazily stirred in his bed on the following morning. He saw in his mind a picture of his uncle's loneliness out here in the house where he and Aunt Alice had spent many happy hours. Perhaps he even sometimes felt her haunting it; she was still perhaps walking up and down the stairs, working in the kitchen and calling out to him as he toiled in the garden. Michael had to admire the courage of his uncle in staying on here, but, after all, it must be the best thing to do.

"He can't wish to leave his memories," he thought, repeating in fact what his father had said. He heard his uncle's footsteps coming from the study past his bedroom So he had been working there for some time already. Michael started up, shot out of bed; he remembered they were going into Presteigne today, and he must be ready on time. He would enjoy looking round this country town which his father had often spoken of with affection. This day promised to be better than yesterday: the sun had broken through the clouds, and the remnants of the storm, the blue reflecting puddles, were part of the haze that in places lent mystery to the green meadows and the line of hedge.

He washed in a most perfunctory way and went downstairs for breakfast. Through the breakfast room window he saw a huge crow tackling a piece of stick on the lawn. Another large crow alighted on the grass and together the two birds bore the stick aloft beyond the boundary of the large garden. Michael shuddered at the thrusting of their aggressive beaks.

"Hurry up Michael or we'll miss the best things in the market," his uncle called. Soon they were in the car driving down the road to Presteigne. They covered the short distance in about fifteen minutes. As soon as they arrived Michael expressed the wish to go to where the old station had been, while his uncle scoured the market for various items.

"Station and track were taken up long ago to build the bypass. As far as I know nothing remains," his uncle informed him. All the same Michael wandered off to try to find any signs of where the track and station had been. He found nothing. They had arranged to meet at a café in the main street should they not meet before, and on the way to the station Michael thought he noticed the girl who had passed him when he had been out posting his letter home. She was on the other side of the street looking in at a shop window.

He sauntered up the main street, looking into various shop windows, a dress shop, fish and chip parlour, fruit shop, a baker's, butcher's and a few pubs, rather a lot for a small town perhaps.

"Nothing much up here," he muttered to himself and decided to find his uncle in the café where they had arranged to meet.

He went back down the main street as the sun grew hotter as midday approached. The shadows grew stronger and stronger in outline, casting ambiguous patterns on the pavement and people moved slowly along in the heat.

His uncle was already in the café and Michael went in to join him. He was surprised to find the girl he had seen sitting with him at the table. He was introduced.

"This is Victoria, daughter of the librarian down the lane," Uncle Hugh said. "And this is Michael, my nephew."

Victoria smiled at him. Michael smiled back into her soft and attractive blue eyes. Her long blond hair fell carelessly over her shoulders. He was pleased to meet such a cheerful girl.

"Are you here for long?" she inquired.

"As long as they'll put up with me," he said.

"Then probably quite long, I think," she replied, still smiling.

That was a nice thing to say and Michael could not help but like her; she was cheerful and in no way deriding as his sister Jane often was.

"Actually I'm waiting for my exam results, keeping my fingers crossed," Michael replied softly.

"Same here," she answered. "I'm trying not to think about it. I want to enjoy my summer holidays."

His uncle bought them both a coffee and a couple of delicious cakes. They chatted happily for a good half hour. Michael was sorry when they took their leave, but probably they'd meet again. She waved goodbye and set off along the road towards King's Turning.

Nevertheless, there was more he wished to explore in the town now that they were there. He thanked his uncle for the coffee and walked up the main street past a few market stands and stopped in front of an old junk shop. He was fascinated by the variety of things he saw in the window: old brasses, an old oil lamp, a leather saddle, a row of books – what was there he couldn't see? He was lucky enough to find a thin dog-eared book giving a short account of the old railway line and a few photographs.

He emerged from the shop, pleased with his purchase.

An elbow nudged him in the back. He turned round to see the face and was not too pleasantly surprised. Surely this was the old man he had encountered in the field at home. At the sight of him Michael sensed uneasily that he had somehow failed that old man - but why should he feel so? He felt all at once the absence of the staff. He had left it behind in his room, unguarded. A sense of responsibility returned, responsibility for the safety of the staff – something he did not own but which was on loan to him and his family for a certain span of time.

He moved awkwardly from side to side under the gaze of this man. He tried to look him in the eye, to answer look with look. But he turned his head away.

"Left behind for others to gather, I suppose?" the old fellow muttered grimly, as though he was expecting nothing better.

"That is how you handle your trust in its last days. When the lease is about to expire, you abandon the property."

"Are you here too?" was all Michael could bring himself to say. He looked at the gnarled weathered brow, the wisps of hair, tousled, unkempt, standing out in random directions as the branches of a tree or bush stick out, according to the whims of nature, the winds and the eccentric growth. The hair was formless, but the eyes, bluer even than when he had last seen him, were fixed on his, flooding Michael's eyes and spreading their hold over his entire face.

"Don't you yet know what to do with it, now the time is drawing to a close?" His voice sang into Michael's ears. He paused, showing his pure white teeth.

"Listen. I shall be off soon before I am seen. Bear the ancient staff of Gwraidd to the entrance of the Hall of the Kings, Hergest Ridge, at Sunday's sunset. Deliver it up to those who are there. Thus it will have a safe return."

He took hold of Michael's arm and pulled him gently to within three inches of his face.

"Make sure this happens, son. Make sure. And keep clear of the dog!"

Michael had expected a threat, but although the old man's eyes were anxious, his voice was pleading. He clung onto his arm and held it tight.

"Let me go! Lay off! Michael whispered furiously. "I'll take the staff back, but let me go!"

"Quiet fool! Don't draw attention. Keep your voice to yourself. The enemy are all around. Do as you are bidden. Go to where I bade you, and beware, the nights are drawing in."

He let go of Michael's arm and shuffled away. Michael jumped as he was suddenly slapped on the back. He turned round, surprised and relieved to see his uncle standing behind him.

"It was nice meeting Victoria, a cheerful uncomplicated young lady."

"Yes, she's nice," replied Michael, "but quick! Who is that old fellow walking off down there?"

"Why that's old Owen, I think, a familiar figure round here, more a tramp than anything else. He's been in these parts, some say, since before the war. He must be knocking eighty."

"Funny, I'm sure I've seen him at home too."

"Hardly possible. He would never get that far. He could never afford to travel. Why should he anyway? When a man's scruffy he looks like any other scruffy old man. You are surely mistaken."

Uncle Hugh changed the subject, telling him about the business he had accomplished that morning; he was especially pleased with the quality of what he had bought, and the farmers he had bumped into were very cheerful because of their high hopes for a good harvest at last, after this long, hot but fairly moist summer."

"Have a look at the paper," and he showed Michael the front page. "Look, there's ill feeling locally at English people buying up old cottages and land in general. It pushes the prices up and makes it hard for our young folk to buy property."

They walked back to the car and set off down the rich green lanes back to the house.

"They mess about with the agriculture and livestock too," continued his uncle. "No feeling for the land."

During lunch neither of them had much to say. His uncle strummed nervously with his large sunburnt hands on the table top, and Michael tried to work out how he should spend the rest of the day. He looked out and cursed silently as it had started to rain again. That meant, he supposed, an afternoon indoors. His head still rang with the words of old Owen that had shot into him like daggers. How could Michael be sure to be on Hergest Ridge on Sunday? What sort of story could he tell to justify being away for dinner? And if it rained as it did now? Perhaps he should say nothing and just stay out sending a message back somehow that he would be late. He hoped to find a public telephone.

After lunch he went up to the library and picked out a book on Welsh legends. The stories were short so that he managed to skip through quite a number: legends of men and women caught in magic circles and disappearing, only to reappear after several decades; tales of ancient kings and kingdoms buried now beneath the soil; and the sea which rose again over the lands in times of crisis; a legend of a maiden who was transformed into a glistening waterfall down the mountainside and emerged later in order to help a youth in time of need; legends of times and ages of yellow and green and an age when the blue of the sky and the rich gold of the land reflected constantly into one another; and of the old king, stripped of his wealth for seven years until.......... Michael nodded off, fast asleep with these fantastic pictures circling round in his mind like planets and comets across the clear night sky.

A barking aroused him. It roared throughout the house, shaking the glass in the cabinet.

"The staff!" he shouted as he leapt up and rushed to his bedroom. It was in an appalling mess, chairs overturned and bedclothes torn off the bed, all soiled by huge paw marks. The staff was gone. Michael dashed to the window as he heard or thought he heard a shrill whistle outside somewhere in the lane. He looked as far as he could down the lane and made out the figure of a man striding briskly off into the distance.

He ran frantically downstairs and down the lane in the pelting rain but saw nothing other than a large black car moving sedately down the main road. Old Owen had warned him in vain. Michael had failed to take enough care. He had been stupidly forgetful. Now he felt truly responsible and guilty. He could not argue himself out of it.

11

He rolled restlessly about in bed. He had sorted his room out as best he could and mentioned nothing to his uncle, though his uncle had of course heard the dog and chased it out, but had evidently not noticed the staff it was carrying. All Uncle Hugh was concerned with was how the animal got into the house. The real worry, that spread out like a threatening hand hovering before his eyes, was of course how to recover the staff. Where had it been taken to? In whose hands was it? How could he track it down? And that large black car, was it involved?

His mind straightaway turned to thoughts of Old Owen, and how he could be at home and here too. For the two men he was thinking about must surely be in fact one man. Why should his errand have become quite suddenly, within the space of a few days, a vital one, one that involved him so fully that it seemed the only thing that mattered?

The only answer was this urgent compulsion in him to recover the staff, as if it were part of his body that had been cut off. Now that it had gone he could scarcely contain anger at his own stupidity in leaving it unguarded. He got up and looked again out of the window. Perhaps he might think more clearly standing up leaning on the sill than lying in bed, though the darkness of the night gave him little to focus his eyes on. His ears caught the gentle rustling of leaves and the swaying of the branches. These soothing sounds helped him to recover some poise, to calm his anxiety that he was mixed up in something he did not understand.

Obviously the next day would be one of seeking, and the day after too, and ... but such thoughts were fruitless and merely created further panic; he must find that black car. Maybe it was still in the neighbourhood. Then he had seen the dog on Bach Hill, so he might start looking there and then wend his way down the other side. He suspected that the dog would be kept on the further side of the hill, otherwise why use the car? That is to say, providing the two were connected.

A further idea crossed his mind: if he had not by dusk on Sunday recovered the staff he should go to the Ridge all the same. Whoever was there might tell him how he could retrieve it. – if there were anyone there. He pondered whether there might be any other clues he could work on, but nothing came to his mind. He returned to bed more at ease, knowing that he could do nothing till daybreak. His thoughts sent him back to a short but fairly deep sleep, strangely uninterrupted by dreams.

Michael felt less alert than usual in the morning and betrayed it by upsetting the milk.

"What on earth's in you this morning?" Kate asked, "you look all glum as though you got out of bed the wrong side."

Michael apologized and went into the dairy to fetch more milk. He cheered up considerably on seeing what a fine day it was: few clouds, a light breeze and plenty of sunshine. The trees cast fine sharp shadows over the lawn and birdsong coloured the landscape with its cheerful, energetic sounds.

"Do you know anyone around here with a black dog, Kate?" he asked, as the elderly woman bent over the grey stone sink. "A scruffy sort of dog, quite big, that is allowed to wander all over the place?"

"Well," she paused, keeping him in suspense, "I don't think I do, really. No black dogs around here, that I know. Anyway, the farmers would be after them if they wandered about. They get at the sheep."

"I wonder if a farmer noticed one in this area yesterday," he thought out loud. He would ask a farmer or a shepherd if he had seen one. He rose from the table and made off, mentioning that he would be back for lunch.

He walked up the hill past Ednol farm in the hope of catching somebody whom he could ask. He thought he had seen someone in the fields the last time he was up in this part. He struggled through hedges and bracken and arrived at the farm, where there was no one to be seen. He walked a little further up the hill; perhaps he would find a shepherd wandering about higher up. Soon he was at the ruined church, and then he stopped with a start. On the large stone where he had sat before Old Owen was now sitting, drawing in the soil with a broken branch. Michael was undecided whether he should turn or approach him. But Old Owen had seen him. He fixed him with his penetrating eyes, opening them wider and wider as his stare became more intense.

"Sit down beside me, fool!" he hissed. "There's a matter we have to talk about, eh?"

Michael drew cautiously near and sat down, fearful, some paces away from the old tramp.

"What do you want?" he stammered. "Why are you here?" The thought flashed through him that he might have the staff.

"The staff! Where is it? Where?" Old Owen wrung his hands at him. "I knew you'd betray us. Can't buckle onto a trust. Bad as the rest of your lot, taking away and not giving back."

"But I didn't know..."

"Find it! Find it! FIND IT!" He shot these words at Michael, like an archer shooting his arrow at a close target.

"Sunday's coming and no staff. The weapon lost! How can a brave army fight?"

"I don't know where to look," Michael pleaded.

"Don't you recognize the sons of darkness? The cottage near the Harley Valley mill – have you not seen them, their dirt and claws?"

He stood up wringing his hands, carried away by the intensity of his feeling.

"Find them. Take back the staff but keep clear of them. If they get hold of you ..." he looked closely at the youth, "they'll change you."

Michael was very anxious at the enormity of the strange task, placed apparently so indiscriminately on his innocent shoulders. He was somewhat indignant too, that it should have come to him.

"Why don't you get it back yourself, if it's yours. Are you afraid?"

Owen reeled back at these words.

"Why, why?" he half sobbed. "I'd redeem it were I only young again; if only I had the trust that you have inherited. My son, don't you learn that your fathers, grandfathers leave you what you never asked for, but what you must accept?"

His eyes sank to the ground where he had traced the signs. His head rose again and held itself aloft in pride and longed-for grandeur. He spoke once more. He did not order: he besought.

"Do not try to understand. Let mind follow heart and guide you there to where your heart can rest and beauty lives. You find and run. Do not fear the hunt. The dogs shall not reach you. Here take this bit of rope." He untied the rope from round his tattered trousers. "Take it, put it round you when in dire straits and you will be safe. You may use it three times. After that it may destroy, so leave it off. You have not yet the strength which you will acquire. Take it and away! With luck you'll be home by noon."

Michael took the rope that was handed to him and stuffed it in his rucksack, making his way downhill and homewards. He was trying to plan what to do and attempting to come to terms with these weird happenings. He would study the map of Harley Valley and work out how long he would need to reach it. He arrived back just after eleven in time to join his uncle in the garden. He was enjoying the good sun and a break from his work.

"Hallo Michael, having a good morning?"

"Yes thank you Uncle," half out of breath., "I was wondering if I could borrow your bike this afternoon, please."

"I don't see why not, if it's in working order. Planning a longer trip?"

Michael told him he wanted to go further afield on a fresh day like this. He was given permission with a warning: the traffic in the area was dangerous in the summer, especially on the A44.

Michael wandered aimlessly round the house and gardens on his own, allowing the latest events to strike him fully after the numbness of their initial impact. He was anxious, apprehensive of the danger he might meet. Then his mind was crossed with anger at the impudent way that dog had invaded the house and run off with his property. But if he took care there would be little danger. Good heavens, it was not a matter of money or gold, just an old carved stick.

He tried to distract himself from all this for a bit, thinking about Victoria. What was she doing now? He liked her and hoped he might see her again.

But he was now quite resolved to go on his little expedition, and returned to the lawn where his uncle was still sauntering about. He asked him what he had been doing that morning and was told that he had been trying to recapture a particular week in 1939 that was fully documented in his diary but which he seemed to have forgotten totally. It was stupid really; Uncle Hugh could no longer see himself on that long hike they had taken over the hills from Rhayader, across the mountains towards an old ruined abbey. In his heart he might remember that week, but it had vanished from his memory.

That week in his life, Uncle Hugh thought, was maybe the key to the past that he was so intent on bringing back to life. Perhaps he would take his nephew back to the scene of part of the hike in a few days' time. Michael hoped he would.

His uncle's face looked strained, the furrows deeper than when he had arrived. Michael worried lest this work were undermining his health. Uncle Hugh was trying to recall a path past rocks beyond an old cottage where he and Alice had spent the night, a path over barren land, where buzzards wheeled high over enormous boulders below.

"Perhaps it'll come back if I work at it," he concluded, and they both strolled into the house for lunch. They ate early, for both had plenty to do.

12

During lunch his uncle spoke about the high land beyond Rhayader, the great preponderance there of rock and stone, left by the retreating ice of that age – a land of desolate, jagged aspect against the otherwise almost total green of the coarse grass. The rough terrain had naturally hindered most sorts of habitation beyond the most primitive and isolated. Occasionally, it is true, one encountered a primitive cottage tucked into a dell with withering trees and rock-filled rough streams for company, all battling against the elements. It was there the old tribes had taken their final refuge before the hordes of invaders, preserving in cases of extreme chance something of themselves till the fury had died down. It was there too that he himself had spent in some isolated cottage that holiday with his wife Alice which he had alluded to and which he now was trying to recall.

He was trying to explain to Michael the frustration felt by older people at the passing of time: they feel, as passing time distances them from an event, this event, though past, will still fill their mind and remain obstinately, often obsessively present. But the great delusion is, and it may need more than a lifetime to come to terms with, that the distance from that event to now is the same as a distance in space where one can turn round and walk back: something that is passed in time is gone for ever and therefore unrepeatable. And yet in our imagination and memory we feel we can touch it.

Michael asked him why then he was trying to repeat it through his writing, and his uncle fell silent. He was unable to answer at once. Michael was embarrassed lest he had hurt his uncle. He was silent too, looking at the softly traced designs on the plates arranged on the huge dresser.

"It is because of the fullness in the past event," his uncle continued slowly and very quietly after a pause. "Certain things you experience, certain times of happiness, fill you so much, make such a deep cut in you, that the cut stays, the fullness remains with you. What *can* you do with it? How can it stay inside you forever? It must not if you are to heal. That is why I'm bringing it out of myself by recording it in writing."

Michael was unable to continue the conversation. His father, his mother never talked like this. He felt he partially understood but needed time to understand fully. He recalled walks he had gone on with a good friend at home when they had tried to discuss deep matters and to elaborate theories about this and that. His experiences here during the past days teemed into his head, but he knew that these were quite different from what Uncle Hugh had been through.

Instead of attempting to answer his uncle he reverted to what he had been told about those ancient tribes that had been driven into the high land: who were they and what had they so desperately tried to preserve?

"Who they were no one knows for certain. Archaeologists could perhaps answer this. All I know is what I suppose from my limited reading: that they took knowledge that they held valuable with them, certain knowledge, for example, how to tame some aspect of nature of which incoming tribes were ignorant."

He stood up, found his pipe, filled it and carried on:

"You see, I'm sure that for every new thing we learn and understand, we lose knowledge and understanding of something we already have. But the newborn baby who replaces the dead old man is no real replacement; the world has lost something unique while it gains something else unique."

Michael's mind had had enough; automatically it flashed over to a different theme with Rhayader as the link: he was thinking of his sister who was supposed to be camping somewhere near this mountain town, and he was wondering whether she was enjoying the life in the open air and the strenuous tasks that were no doubt being forced upon her. He smiled. His uncle got up to get back to his work and Michael rose too.

"All the best for your work, Uncle Hugh,. I must be off."

"Watch it on that bike," Uncle Hugh warned again, "and watch those motorists who rage along with no concern for man or beast."

"Which of the two do you think I am?" Michael grinned and hurried off to the shed to collect the bike. He was fit and used to cycling at home and set off fast down the lane and in no time had turned left and was pedalling furiously down the main road, slackening pace only when he heard a lorry coming or when the strong sun beat down on his forehead.

Gradually he was adjusting himself to his task for the afternoon – the dog, or failing that, the black car – the dog, black all over, light brown eyes, large teeth with a savage bark, dirty looking and thoroughly nasty. He shuddered, hot as he was, at the thought of having to touch such a beast. No friendly people would keep such an animal. He passed through Kinnerton, past the field where he had seen the Four Stones and on down the road to New Radnor. He had just come into New Radnor and was pedalling down the main street when he was almost frightened over the kerb by an army lorry as it roared past him presumably on its way to the coast.

Apart from that New Radnor in the afternoon was almost as quiet as a churchyard at night. No other traffic passed him as he dismounted and walked along. Now was the time to finalize his plans. He hid his bike in the churchyard and set off on foot with the open map in his hands. He felt the fieldglasses jogging about in his rucksack as he walked and felt the rope that Old Owen had given him safe inside it. He walked up the hillside some distance away from the road but parallel to it. Very soon he came to clumps of bracken so situated that crouching behind it he was afforded a good view onto the road and onto the house along it. He looked very carefully through the glasses and sighted the two houses that Old Owen could have been referring to. Outside one of them a man was sawing wood over a bench, and was now and then reaching out for something, a cup of tea perhaps. The other house seemed without life and in neither property did he see a dog. He was glad of the glasses for he was able to scour the land round about in detail. All the same he found nothing significant. He sat down and gazed around aimlessly, reaching out to the hedge to snap off a hazel stick.

His thoughts went back to the Four Stones and the strange experience he had had there in the full sun. Then all at once he was alerted by the aggressive barking of a dog. Down on the road he spotted his prey, quite clear in the glasses, a wild black beast jumping up at a passing cyclist. What a relief that he had left his bike in the churchyard.

He gathered his things together quickly and slithered stealthily down the slope, keeping the dog carefully in view. To which house if either did it belong? No one left either house to restrain it as it leapt madly at the poor innocent cyclist. Then quite abruptly it dashed into the garden of the other house, where there was apparently nobody. Within a second a woman shot out by a side door and dragged the animal inside.

"Who the hell let him out?" she shouted in a loud, raw voice.

Michael shuffled further down the slope, sure that he had found his enemy. He kept low, making certain he could not be seen from below. He hid the rucksack in the bracken and crept on his belly through the ferns till he reached the hedge bordering the garden. Should he break in and see what he could find? The woman had seemed as gruff and as nasty as the dog. He was afraid. But then, if he were found and handed over to the police he was sure he could make out a good case for being where he was, and Uncle Hugh would corroborate that the dog had broken into his house even though Michael had kept quiet about the theft of the staff. He was annoyed that the creature had been able under his very nose to steal that staff and make off with it unmolested.

He found a gap in the hedge and crept into the garden. He still kept very low, making his way round the greenhouse, along a wall with just one side window. He bit his lip in anger as he realized he had left the rope behind in the rucksack; he might as well try it, and it was with relief that he had found an excuse to leave these premises. He crept uphill to the rucksack, pulled out the rope, tied it round his waist and re-entered the garden. He had doubted the old man's words and feared that the rope would do nothing for him but compound the fear he had already. He had been silly to waste time fetching it.

Now the dog had begun to bark, so he had probably been spotted. The woman rushed out of the house looking in all directions. Michael stood still and quiet against the wall. She came round the corner to where he was, a woman of about forty, with heavily made-up face and long painted fingernails. She looked straight at him and through him!

"She can't see me!" was the first thought that sprang to his mind and disbelieving what had happened to him. He dared to stand to look through the window as the woman returned to the front of the house. He looked into what must be the larder; the glass was frosted, so he saw little. He heaved himself carefully onto an outside sill and peered in through a higher open window.

On the shelf before him lay the staff! It was incredible that those who had stolen it had been so stupid as not to hide it in some deep chest amongst a hundred discarded items of clothing; but maybe these thieves understood the staff far better than he did, perhaps in a strange way it needed the fresh air and the light of the sun to keep its charm alive, whatever that was. Michael did not know. The pressing issue was: could he reach it and recapture it? The woman dashed out again, looking frantically round her, but did not see the youth extending his arm to grasp what she must have thought secure. He took the staff to his own again. It seemed to sweat and grow warm as he held it, and even throbbed a little as if sap were rising inside it. It might have been flesh as his hand now sensed it. He pulled himself out of the window and jumped down as he heard the dog scratching and yelping at the larder door. Michael started for the hole in the hedge and at that moment the woman rushed into the garden screaming:

"Rats! Rats! They're here, the thieves. Get them!"

She had seen the footprints Michael had left on breaking through the hedge on the first occasion. Michael tried to race her to the gap, but she was there first, well knowing that something was up. He took the risk and tried to brush invisibly past her. She did not see him, but she felt him and caught him, pressing him violently against her in an attempt to hold him while she called for help. He felt the wild sweating warmth of her breast heaving excitedly, as her arms clasped him more and more tightly, pushing him more and more into her own body. She was searching with one hand for the rope, tied like a belt round his waist, trying to loosen it. Michael kicked her hard on the shin and pushed her over, falling on top of her as he desperately tried to break free from her grasp.

"You little devil. I'll teach you a lesson when I unmask you," she panted. "I'll have that belt off. I know where you got it from."

He pushed his hands into her painted powdered face and broke free just as a man emerged from the house. In a trice Michael was through the hedge and up the hill with the staff and the rope safe in his possession. Now the dog was out too and chasing him. Michael swung the staff at the dog and the beast retreated, yelping, back into the garden.

"Stop thief!" the man yelled, but Michael was no longer afraid. They could not catch him and the dog who could follow his scent was too frightened to do so. He retrieved his rucksack and made his way rapidly towards the churchyard, the woman's loud gruff voice still resounding in his ears.

"We will find you! We know where!"

Her voice filled Michael with loathing. He felt a sharp pain on his neck, touched it and found blood on his fingers where she must have bitten him in the struggle or scratched him with her long pointed fingernails. He held the warm vibrating staff very tightly.

13

Michael was safe from his enemies for a short time only. He heard a car engine revving up about a hundred feet below him as it backed cautiously out of the dilapidated wooden garage onto the main road.

He climbed over the stone wall on the hillside and kept close to it as he approached the walled churchyard where he had left his bike. It was still leaning against the wall invisible from the road.

"Hullo, enjoying a cycling holiday?" he shot round alarmed, reassuring himself that the rope was still round his waist. It was. And he could be seen after all. The parish rector was speaking from the church porch, complete in black suit and dog collar.

"Er, I hope you don't mind. I left my bike here against the wall while I went for a walk. I thought it would be safe here."

The rector was unconcerned about the bike, interested only in Michael's holiday, whether he was enjoying it, where he had come from and was cycling to. Michael answered briefly, giving no more information than necessary, stealing frequent anxious glances in the direction of the roadway lest the enemy should espy him. The rector complained about the noisy traffic and pointed down to the road while Michael tried to conceal himself from it. His voice droned on in Michael's ears about the noise of cars and how the countryside was changing for the worse, when Michael with a start noticed his pursuers looking up towards the churchyard. He saw the dog, its head poking out of the car window, sniffing at the air.

"Those people down there are not too popular here either," the rector continued in his loud Welsh voice. "They don't take to our ways and want to alter things."

The couple were still scouring the hillside carefully. Surely they were looking up in this direction. The man was holding binoculars to his eyes, but he obviously did not see Michael. At least that's what he concluded when the car started off down the road towards the village centre.

Michael wondered whether to them he was still quite invisible – that is to say, judging from their last actions. Consequently he felt more at ease while chatting with the rector: he remarked that he did not like those people either. They had the habit of driving over the whole area and seemed to be very inquisitive about other people's business. He mentioned where he was staying on the off chance that he might know Hugh Pritchard his uncle. However, the rector did not know him, adding that it was outside his parish.

"Perhaps we'll meet again," he said bidding Michael goodbye. He went back into the church and Michael wheeled his bike cautiously down the path and onto the road. He was willing to chance the fact that he was invisible to that man and woman and possibly to their dog also. Maybe the rector saw him through some power peculiar to a priest of the Church. Old Owen's rope was indeed even more remarkable if it made him invisible only to his enemies. Nevertheless, he took a roundabout route back to his uncle's. He turned down a side lane and consulted the map in an obscure corner. His prime concern was how to guard against a second loss of the staff, and a bright idea came to him and he bent over the map. Why not hide the staff somewhere out here in the wilds, somewhere preferably that lay between Hergest Ridge and his uncle's?

His eyes moved along the road to Kinnerton and then right, down the narrow lane to the Four Stones. The Four Stones! Just the place to hide this ancient staff, as long as he could find some cranny or hole that could take it. He looked at the staff in his hand and it appeared to be changing: firstly its colour – surely it had lost the dead brown aspect and was becoming green, as though the sap were somehow returning. And the knot of cut-off twigs along it – surely there was a suggestion of green tips beneath the gnarls? Perhaps this was only his overactive imagination, as his mother, or more likely his sarcastic sister might have put it; but was the staff not straighter and very slightly longer than when he had first taken it? He visualized it hanging on the lounge wall at home. No, it had not been that long then, he was sure.

Michael decided therefore to hide it beneath one of the stones and to collect it from there on his way to the Ridge, that he might have it safely for dusk on Sunday. He found a track on the map, narrow between two hedges; that was the shortest and safest way to the stones from where he was now. He pushed his bike cautiously onto the main road and moved quickly towards the gap where the track started.

At that moment a black car with dirty, yellowed windows, emitting clouds of fumes from the exhaust, drove past him. His pursuers again, but once more they had missed him. He checked on the rope: it was tight round his waist.

The path was moist after the rains, especially where the sun had not penetrated and driven the moisture into the air. His shoes became quite wet even after a short distance. He cursed the various holes and ditches on the path which prevented him constantly from looking ahead. He stopped for a minute to try to recognize where he was going. Before him lay a length of undulating hills separating Wales from England, the named ridges all studded with the various greens of larch, pine and broadleaf and the odd bright yellow of flowering bushes. Small streams dashed down to underlay the fields with constant moisture, to give shape to the hillsides and a growth to hedgerows and to single trees that stood so splendidly on this small plain – the drinking fields of Radnorshire, Maesyfed as the Welsh call it. There; he had retained something of what he had been reading. The sight of these ancient hills and the mysterious track along and between them roused him, and he knew not whether it was he himself or the staff that urged him on.

Within twenty minutes he was at the gate to the field with the Four Stones. As a precaution he pulled the bike over the gate with him before seeking out the best hiding place, he moved away with his hands the earth from under the most slanting of the stones, the stone that slanted in line with the row of trees two fields away, and with the incline of Whimble Hill. He knew how long the staff was but was encouraged by the softness of the earth. After he had dug about a foot with his bare hands he felt open space beneath a shaft that went down beyond where he could reach, and from the shaft poured sweet, perhaps scented air, and there was a suggestion of sound, of a song that rose and fell in waves like the hills around. He pushed the staff down the hole, lodging it carefully lest it fall too far for him to retrieve when the hour came. He replaced the bit of turf he had removed over the hole and went for his bike. How should he avoid those people again on his way home? They would be blocking his way somewhere, he was sure.

He took his bike which he had concealed behind the largest stone and felt it vibrate at his finger tips. The singing, which just now had only been suggested, now rose confidently from the ground beneath the stones. It was a solo voice, noble, young, full of vigour, but singing in sorrow as if in tones of long ago. It was as if it were the land about him singing. He fell into a dream of old castles, white-clad knights moving around lofty pillars, hewn from a mass of granite. He took hold of the handlebars of the bike and the song gradually died away, the dream was gone, and so to some extent were his fears of being trapped on the way home. He knew the staff was safe and knew too of a way round to the back of his uncle's house that avoided the lane.

He passed the lane down to the house and sure enough, the black car was parked halfway along it, waiting. He went to Lower Litton where he turned left down a track that passed at a small distance that house where Victoria must live, for he thought he saw her entering her house from the garden; he recognized her long blond hair. The track led further to the gate between those tall swaying trees at the end of Hugh's back garden. He pushed open the gate and put the bicycle in the shed. He went cautiously, keeping out of sight from the lane and entered the house. His heart leapt as at the last minute he remembered to remove the rope and hide it in his room before others saw it. He decided, however, at last to tell his uncle a little of what had happened, that he too might help to keep his pursuers at bay.

"Had a good day?" his uncle greeted him. You've taken quite a tan. And you're just in time for dinner."

14

At dinner that evening his uncle seemed more relaxed than Michael had known him this holiday. His worn face smiled benignly at his nephew as he pulled his leg about the reasons for Michael staying out for so long.....So he had come past the back of Victoria's garden! Maybe he had spent more time there than he wanted to say! He smiled again as Michael tried to conceal his embarrassment. However, he was really far more interested in what Michael had been doing during his day out.

"Here, come on and have a second helping of this delicious Herefordshire beef, as long as you save some space for the ice cream and raspberries to follow. What have you been doing today then? You seemed a bit harassed when you came in."

All the same Michael appreciated the interest his uncle was taking. He told him about the couple in the black car, and in modified terms of his struggle with them. Uncle was sure they were the same man and woman who had driven slowly and inquisitively past the house that afternoon. An unsavoury couple, he added, but Michael need not be worried by them, just try to keep out of their way.

Yet Michael was certain they would follow him around and plague him, and he did not tell his uncle about how the staff had been stolen and of its retrieval. That might seem almost like burglary. He was still naturally in fear and said so.

"I think they'll be after me here. They want something from me, I'm sure. Please say nothing if they ask about me."

"Now Michael, what makes you think I'd betray you, especially to folk such as those? They're newcomers here who would turn the place upside down if they could."

His uncle stared a few minutes into his beer glass, then turned again to Michael.

"Sure you're not imagining the whole thing? Sounds a bit far-fetched to me. What can they be wanting from you?"

Michael fell silent. Perhaps it would be best to reveal nothing further.

"It's just a feeling I have that they think I have something of theirs. The man looked at me as though I was a thief," he added some moments later.

"Some people look like that naturally. I shouldn't worry, and if you are frightened of them, keep well out of their way. Myself, I feel you read too much into that dog breaking into the house."

He changed the subject and started to reminisce about his days here before the war when he and his wife had walked out further into the hills westwards, until it seemed they had left the world of men behind. Yes, he was planning to go back there some day soon and retrace their steps – it might even be in these holidays if the weather held and things seemed right for it. They could leave the car just past Rhayader and walk from there to save time. He was determined to find the path that he and Alice tried to follow. To see where it went and whether it was still traceable. He wanted to see whether the track led to a small isolated glen sheltering fine trees and ancient parkland and an old house that had once been a homestead.

Michael half listened. Through his sleepy eyes he could see the trees at the end of the garden swaying very gently in the evening breeze, and the strange blues that the sky offered, coming through the trees where the foliage was not too thick. Beyond the trees he saw cattle moving all in one direction up the slope of the hill.

His uncle continued talking of that holiday so long ago under circumstances so different. He mentioned the flat and undulating land on the top of the hills, of the gulleys that maintained maybe one battered tree, of the rocks scattered at random and of the few sheep wandering noiselessly over the rugged slopes. It was that past life within him that he was attempting to coax out with words, a fire that had died, died but which his frame had absorbed and wished to rekindle. Michael stirred himself to keep awake as the cows vanished from the view outside. He wanted to change the subject despite his obvious interest.

"I'd like to see that landscape, Uncle, but perhaps," he paused, a little nervous, "you could tell me about Hergest Ridge; I'd like to go there by myself tomorrow, if that's all right."

"Fascinating up there on the Ridge. The long plateau stretches for some distance south-west till it narrows down to the Ridge proper. At its furthest extremity stands a bent old yew tree, a half-dead watchman at the end looking down to the hamlet of Gladestrey. The village of Hergest is on the south-east side. There, it is supposed, the *Red Book of Hergest* had its origin, one of the old books of Welsh legends that go back to the days of the Holy Grail, King Arthur and further back to the prehistoric times of Owain ar Iriodd, the hero who established and maintained the world's balance, safe-guarding it from falling off its path and plunging into chaos. Even today he is needed."

Michael's attention was strongly caught as a bush is seized by the wind and struggles not to be torn from its roots by the wind's enthusiasm. He indicated that he wanted to hear more.

"... On the top of the Ridge are those mysterious stones. Some say they are all that is left of the old temple where the rites connected with the Grail were observed before the invading Anglo-Saxon tribes obliged the Celts to retreat underground or further west in order to preserve their heritage. The brotherhood grew smaller and smaller till few remained. Who knows whether today any are left or whether all have been driven into the sea?"

Michael recalled the ancient brotherhoods he had read of somewhere when younger and the secret societies he had formed with his school friends in a kind of impious imitation. His uncle was pleased to have captured his attention so thoroughly, and with almost malicious delight he continued:

"The sworn brotherhood have or had a most sacred task: to keep secure these ancient secrets till a better time when they can be enjoyed generally in the world of men and no longer need remain secrets."

He paused to fill his pipe.

"So you see Michael you will be treading on hallowed ground when you go up there."

"What is the Grail, Uncle?"

"The sacred cup of life, drunk from by many holy men since the earliest times and lastly by Jesus at the Last Supper. Only he who has been vouchsafed a vision of the world beyond the world may safely drink from it. At other times it was exposed, held up for adoration by those who understood."

"So an old temple stood on Hergest Ridge."

"Some say so. I cannot prove it, but when you go up there you will see the stones and see how the Ridge seems to be a heart, the central point of converging rings from all compass points. You'll take the bike, I suppose; it's quite a way on foot."

"I'd like to, please, if you're not using it."

"Well, I must get upstairs to carry on. You may like to browse along the bookshelves for further information on these old legends. There'll be some truth in them, I daresay, but truth is a strange phenomenon: things are often true in a way other than how we imagine."

He went out through the door leaving Michael to sort out his remark. On his way upstairs he was stopped by Kate who called up to him.

"There's a man at the door, Mr Pritchard, who wants to speak to Michael. Would you please come down and see him. There's something I don't like ..."

Uncle Hugh seemed annoyed at the interruption. He strode to the front door as Michael, picking up what he had said, stared anxious but curious through the half-open door. He heard the voice of the man who had been pursuing him but could not see him, for his uncle's body obscured the smaller body of his adversary. The man was insisting on speaking to Michael but would give no plausible reason. Uncle Hugh was impatient and in a loud voice he dismissed the man.

"I am certainly admitting no one to speak to him unless he has a sound reason. I can't understand why you should wish to worry the lad. Please go."

He shut the door and a few seconds later Michael heard the car door slam shut and the car drive off.

"Keep out of that fellow's way," was all his uncle said as he climbed the stairs to his study.

Michael went up to the library, trembling but relieved. The staff was safe, only he knew where it was hidden. He leant out of the window and saw the car turn into the road at the bottom of the lane and heard its rough engine change gear as it moved off fast. The sound of the car died away and quietly, very quietly, from somewhere near the horizon, from over the hilltop perhaps, he heard a gentle singing voice, the tender voice of a young woman. The soft blues of the sky that melted so gradually into the grey and white of cloud might have been moving too in time with these almost silent reverberations.

15

The singing echoed within his head as he browsed through the variety of books of legends and pored over maps ancient and new of the area. He found next to nothing of what his uncle had told him. Where had he derived such information, he asked himself. The prospect of standing on Hergest Ridge seized him now suddenly with awe, with the sensation that he was embarking on something too big for him alone to manage. The gravity of his task was taking hold of him. All that had happened to him rose to the surface of his mind and flowed down his neck to fill out his limbs and muscles – and the soft voice, was that too part of his memory? Surely it was, along with the old man, the story of how the staff had come into the possession of his family, and the particularity of this summer of all summers, of the Four Kings' stones and the voices from beneath the earth, as nature herself shaped the fields, woods and paths with wind, rain and fine-hewn stones. Behind all this lurked the fear of pursuit by the people outside and their savage dog. There it was now, barking away in some lane not so far away. Michael took the rope and hid it for the night beneath the mattress.

How his sister would mock him if he attempted, foolishly of course, to tell her of these adventures!

He slept, and in his dream eyes he saw many rocks rising high as they built the landscape and the water tumbling down and between them as hair tresses fall over elegant shoulders. The bird that had seized the branch to devour it was drawing back, and soon the tree would be exposed to full view again. The branches would all balance out and the structure would not fall. It would stand, and she with the flowing white dress and golden blond hair over it would emerge to greet him, her eyes shining in the dawn light.

So despite the howling of the dog he slept to wake strong from his wonderful dreams. Jack, however, had been kept awake hours by that dratted dog and was prepared to shoot it. So was his uncle. Both were determined to catch the blighter and shut it up somewhere till they could cart it off some distance away.

"Morning Michael," his uncle greeted him as he came downstairs, "I see our friends have left their visiting card. So as not to lose it we'll have to put it in a very safe and secure place."

Michael was relieved to have allies. He had been racking his brains as to how to evade that animal. He had no guarantee that it would not follow his scent, even though the rope would render him invisible. Uncle Hugh assured him that Jack was quite capable of trapping it to lock it up in the shed for twenty-four hours, giving them time to dispose of it as they felt fit.

"And if it insists on barking all the time we'll give it some carefully prepared food to quieten it. Don't worry, your trip to the Ridge, if you want to go today, will be unimpeded."

Michael went upstairs to plan the route he would be taking later; he would not have to set out too early to reach the Ridge by dusk, and yet two things had to be considered: he had to retrieve the staff on the way and had to be sure he did not set out too late for his uncle to point out that he would never reach the Ridge and be back again before dusk. He would have to deceive his uncle but only in a mild sort of way; he would give him to understand that he would arrive back at the usual time for dinner, and then explain why he was late when he failed to return as he had said.

He heard a sudden flareup of mad barking, followed by a shout of triumph.

"All right Michael! All clear. He's locked up in the shed and won't be out in a hurry."

Michael was now concerned lest they might be expecting him to leave in the morning. He explained that he had not planned the trip till the afternoon and spent the rest of the morning on the hill at the back of the house reading and surveying the landscape. He waved to Victoria as she came out into the garden to call her brother in. Looking down at her the vision in his dreams flashed momentarily across his mind. It was her blond hair and shining blue eyes, no doubt.

All seemed safe outside. Nothing to alarm him. No sign of the enemy. He returned promptly for lunch, and after lunch packed his rucksack with a few provisions and made sure the rope was safely tucked into his pocket. He would use it only in emergency.

"I thought you were leaving earlier than this," Uncle Hugh remarked. "Make sure you're back before sunset; the bike has poor lights."

Michael tried to reassure him without becoming involved in a deliberate lie. As a precaution he put a torch in his pocket that he found by the front door. He said goodbye and left the premises by the back path over the hillside to Lower Litton. He took a roundabout route to avoid the road to Kinnerton, which meant wheeling the bike arduously for some distance. He walked along Offa's Dyke path, glancing round him on all sides for the enemy. He saw nothing to trouble him save perhaps for one moment when he espied a man curiously upright on a white horse, going in the same direction as he moved along a hillside some quarter of a mile away to his left. Then the figure disappeared as the sun shone down on the calm deep forests of the borderland, making the green light they reflected rise just perceptibly into the warmer atmosphere of the wide plain.

The sunlight reflected into his eyes in such a way as to make him turn his head and look forward there to the right, to those Four Stones, guardians of the kings and the staff of generations. He hid deeply in the bracken till he judged the time right for him to retrieve the staff. He read the map again and ate some of the food he had, whiling away the time until the sun was lower and consequently less bright. He made his way carefully with the bike towards the Stones and brought out the staff intact, quite unobserved in the stillness of the early evening. His hands and nails were gritty with the work.

The staff clung hard to his hand and seemed to be urging him along on his journey towards the Ridge as a water diviner's stick pulls towards the place where water is. The staff was now he estimated over five feet long, grown taller and more significant than when he had last held it, more worthy than ever to be safeguarded and returned to its rightful home.

He moved out of the field and left the road as soon as he could; he had heard a car coming and had grown alarmed. He struggled further with the bike around fields, along paths, across meadows with frisky cattle, bumping the back wheel over stones and clumps as he rode over the rough ground.

At Lower Harpton he crossed a road and grew alarmed at the speed of the sinking sun, blazing down towards the horizon like a huge shield. He rode off furiously down the main road. Another car was coming. He dashed through a gate as it sneaked round the bend, an old black car. Their car? He was taking no chances, lying prostrate in the field as it rattled past.

He was soon on his bike again speeding towards the Ridge, towards the ascent, holding the staff securely like a lance over the handlebars. He was forced to dismount and walk up an old tractor track. He passed a tumbledown shed and decided to leave the bike in it. The sun's rays were now like a sharp sword blade glinting over the horizon, but as he climbed its full body came once more into view. He climbed, a warrior with his staff, alone to meet his destiny. Then quite suddenly he emerged from the diverse clumps of bracken and gorse onto a wide plain, the top of the Ridge, a space void of bush and tree, bare but for the grass and wild stacks of stones. And was that a rider coming over there ahead of him, the figure he had glimpsed briefly that afternoon?

The sun dropped and he automatically lowered the staff before him, standing easy and still as the strange mists, that surround all when they stand here at sundown or when they recall the landscape of the past, the strange white mists rise, and the figures of horses white and brown move towards a central point. A chill rose from the ground. Michael shuddered, and as he shuddered that weird music began and was part of the landscape, mist and horse-tread, the music of the ancient Kings' Stones. He moved forward towards what he sensed was the highest point, the staff high before him, and the horses that must have surrounded him moved forward too. The staff clung tightly to his hand.

In front of him he saw a mound of stones. They looked as though they were the remains of some former lofty building, long since fallen from its rounded pillars and square stone walls. The horses round him drew nearer, snorting loudly as if impatient for what was to happen, prancing excitedly and blowing out from their nostrils, these elegant beasts now so clear to his eyes.

To his right the mists were rising and the music too, and now in the moonlight the silver circle which it cast on the earth, he saw a ring of flowers, white circles, touched with red in their centres. And towards this ring he moved; the staff pulled him thither.

He was standing in the centre of the ring, the staff at his side. No flower had been touched. The mists rose higher still and the light of the moon transformed all hues, so that they appeared to transcend normal colours. On the far western horizon a dim red lantern in this light, was the vanishing sun, its last light. The silver-white horses reared up as its final rays quickened their eyes. He saw the riders, tall and majestic in procession, moving in shapes and patterns against sky and earth. One of them dismounted and strode in white flowing garments towards him. It was perhaps the mist itself that was wrapped around him. Michael looked into his face and through the staff reached a recognition: it was Old Owen, or the once Old Owen, for now he walked erect and in the fullness of manhood towards him, proud and regal.

"You have come then, young man, and the staff of Peredur is with you. The time of lease is over and we take from you the trust you have bravely borne and your ancestors before you. Look, the procession all moves towards this point!"

He waved his arm gracefully around him and Michael saw the people of his world converge and halt. He raised his head and beheld in front of him the noblest of the assembled company.

"There stands the King to take our homage. We are all his vassals."

Owain's words fell and rose with the song that moved behind them. Michael saw the lofty building rise high into the mist so that its roof was lost. The doors were opening for all to enter this high palace! On either side of the doors stood warriors who guarded it, and from them fanned out two lines of silver-armoured knights. All stood still as statues in attendance on their King.

"Go forward, young man. Present him with the staff." Owain whispered in his ear. Michael dared not move. He tried to step forward and managed to raise a foot slowly, fearfully. The mists pressed on his forehead. The immense expanse of bright light was blinding him. He was holding the staff so tight, that it was as if it were rooted to his hand. The mists rose further, oppressing his ears and pressing on the top of his head. The whiteness was going to the relief of his eyes, but greyness followed and then there was black, darkness around him. He looked round for Owen but saw nothing. There was only dull silence and a totally black night.

Terror seized him, alone and so cold on the dark hill without clear knowledge of the descent. He was trapped and might never get back that night; he might be lost, in grave danger, with no one to help him. Suddenly alone on this empty inhospitable ridge. He yelled out but the damp air was a cushion in his mouth. The staff grew limp in his hand. He ran down the hill where he thought he had come up. He soon reached a road and was grateful to a couple who offered him a lift in their car.

16

"Here, drink this, drink this nice warm cocoa. You've had a nasty shock. You're suffering from exposure. You're so cold you might be a corpse. Drink, you'll soon feel better."

A woman leaned over him as he sat exhausted in the back seat and let the staff fall to the ground. He looked up at her and saw the patternless lines, the wrinkles on her face. He saw her and he froze, colder and colder. Then the cocoa filled his throat and he drank, looking into her shallow lustreless eyes. He fell into a half-conscious slumber as the car rumbled on, driven by the short-necked small man in front with the rigid head concentrating fanatically on its task.

Michael's head swirled, turning faster and faster like a top being whipped, till from sheer speed all seemed to stand still on a plain far above where he was now. He was in a dream-world: the summit of the hill was vacant, so empty that he thought he would have to run, gasping for twenty or thirty miles to reach the rock ahead of him. The faster he ran the further away it was, yet it did not move. It was a thing that could not be reached with this sort of movement. Maybe it should never be reached, for it was a bare inhospitable-looking rock, a mass of stone with nowhere to cling on to. He ran slower and slower till he was no longer moving forward despite the effort his legs were making. He stopped still, his head expanding like a balloon being blown up by forces outside. His eyes swelled. He could not close them to shut out the desolation around him. He heard the old man's voice crying in his ears:

"Fool! Fool! Fool!"

He woke up and was violently sick. He was lying in a shed on a damp bed of straw. It had evidently been raining very heavily and the rain had seeped in under the rotten substructure of the shed. His arms and feet were bound, allowing him some movement, but nevertheless quite firmly bound. He was a prisoner, he knew to his horror, as he slowly revived and assessed his situation. Dreams and half-dreams, mixing shaped and violent colours – never still – shot through his mind as he tried to focus on some external point and wriggle out of the mess he had made.

He felt first the fears that grasped him here alone and preyed upon his mind as the ignorance of his bearings preoccupied him more. He was hungry, thirsty, helpless and very cold. Winter had come into his body. He dozed a while till his discomfort wrenched him awake. He recalled being on Hergest Ridge, present at some awesome spectacle, and then the mists and light that blinded him from all round, the mists too in his body that paralysed him, struck in that cold fear. Finally the flight. Then back to the words of Old Owen, and the staff...where was it, the staff he had guarded, hidden and retrieved from the Stones of the Kings? He had failed. He had lost the object of his Sunday journey. In vain he scoured the ground around him, but no staff. That he had lost, and its rightful owners too, they were gone... taken from him by the machinations of his enemies. He groped as he could around all corners of the shed, but fell back in the horror that he could do nothing. He was helpless and unable to act.

He sat trembling for what must have been hours. No one came to him. He slept and woke but still no one came. And he was so hungry and thirsty. It grew darker and colder. He was shivering and starting to feel tearful. Why should anyone do this to him? What had he done to merit it?

"There are three things we want from you," said a voice over him. "One we have already, the others we shall get. Firstly where is our dog? Towser, dear Towser, such a playful fellow, a man's faithful friend. My wife is quite distraught. You don't want to stay here any longer, do you? We hate doing this to you, but we must find our dog and, of course, that old tramp – we have to find him too. It upsets us, all this, as I am sure it upsets you; but you'll help us, won't you?"

"I don't know where your dog is. You can see I haven't got him. I'm surprised he's not sniffing at the door now, the way you've been sending him after me. Untie me and please let me go. I do not understand what you want, so how can I help you?"

Michael was inwardly amazed that such defiant words came from his mouth.

"Are you trying to bargain with us, young man?" The man in the neat blue suit reacted sternly to Michael's response.

"Listen. You tell us what we want to know and you go free. That is our bargain. We have no wish to hurt you, but if you insist on treating us as enemies, you'll just stay here, and there's no telling what we could do to a young lad like you."

He looked at Michael with his hard blue eyes. Michael returned the look and felt his headache getting worse from that hard, cold stare.

"What about the dirty old tramp then?" the man continued. "You do know where we can find him. You see, there are dangerous people about and we are out to stop them. You can help to stop these folk wrecking the country, prevent them holding up progress," his mouth tightened as he spoke almost without moving his lips, "progress on which we all depend."

Michael moved his glance from the man's eyes to his sleek, well-oiled black hair. The man was still screwing his eyes into him.

"That old tramp may seem harmless, but he is not. We are investigating his affairs and wish to speak with him."

"How can I tell you where to find him? You know just as well as I do where he is. He's a tramp and that means he's always wandering about. How can I know where he is if he's never in one place?"

Michael secretly congratulated himself on his well-reasoned answer, but it annoyed the man even more.

"I told you, you make no bargains. You know of two or three places where we might find him. Where did he give you that staff anyway?"

"No one gave it to me. It belongs to my family, and I'll have it back if you please. You took it from me."

With difficulty he refrained from mentioning the word 'thief'; he did not wish unnecessarily to annoy his captors. But the man forced his scowl into a wrinkled grin, which looked somehow worse.

"*Your* staff? You silly fool! *Your* staff? You ignorant schoolkid."

He threw Michael an apple and a packet of biscuits, placed a bottle of water on the floor as he left the shed.

"I'll be back later when you've changed your mind."

He closed and locked the shed door, leaving Michael in almost complete darkness. Michael rolled across the floor and grasped the apple. After a few contortions he managed to take a few bites. The biscuits were easier to get at, and he had soon eaten those he had scattered on the floor. He grabbed the unstoppered bottle in his teeth, tipped it up and gulped the water that did not spill over his clothes. He was still feeling ill and disgusted that the man had made no attempt to clean up the mess he had made on the floor. He had showed no concern at all for his sick state.

He was now less hungry and able to understand better the gravity of his predicament. The dominant feeling was shame: that he had failed to deliver up the staff and had lost it to the hands of alien forces. Yes, he was certain they were alien, more certain than ever. He resented the man's assumption that he would betray someone just because he was a tramp. The shame at failure gripped him more powerfully than his woeful situation. In losing the staff it was as if he had lost part of himself, a part that had given him importance and a task that stretched beyond the everyday.

The words of Old Owen: "Fool! Fool! Fool!" grated on his mind.

His thoughts turned to his uncle and how worried he must be. Michael had been out for hours longer than he had said, a whole day even. He grew very agitated and struggled to free his hands but the rope only cut tighter into him. He struggled to his feet and tried to loosen the ropes there, but all he managed to do was hop around the shed. After several minutes he gave up, exhausted and feeling forced to remain on the ground.

The shed door opened and a woman entered. She looked sheepishly at him and spoke in a soft lulling voice, the voice he had heard all those hours ago in the car. He looked into her intense close-set brown eyes and her body in a tight sweater and trousers. Her face was elaborately made up; the dark red lipstick emphasized her lips, and as she talked gently she played with her tongue in the corner of her mouth. Michael felt compelled to listen to the tone of her voice and stare at her face rather than take in what she was saying. She was quietly pitying yet at the same time despising him, and he was uncertain as to how to respond.

She continued: "My husband's spoken to you, hasn't he? Now don't get upset. Did he say something to upset you? Oh dear, he's often so tactless. Why can't we both tell him to use more tact? You know, I've told him so often; it seems to have no effect. I suppose he's already put you against us ... the enemies' best weapon, surely he is. Well look, dearie, all I ask is that you help us just this little bit in our investigations. It may not seem very much, but you could help if you answered our questions."

She stopped, stooped down to him and stroked his face with her hand. Michael felt her painted nails graze slightly against his skin. He shuddered.

"You'll listen to me and help, won't you?"

She held him loosely by the arm. Michael winced. He could smell her, the sickly perfume coming from her body.

"I feel sick. Let me out of here." He turned away and vomited on the floor.

"Set me free," he gasped.

She was unsympathetic.

"Of course. Come on now, you do look bad. Just a couple of words and you're free."

"Set me free. I am ill and in pain tied up here."

"Of course, if that's what you want, Michael. That is your name, isn't it? You don't mind me knowing?"

She helped him up and dragged him out of the shed. They would talk matters over somewhere more comfortable, she assured him. She put her arm round his waist and guided him as he hopped along past the door of the house. She tapped on the window. The man came out and they both pulled Michael towards some shrubbery at the end of a narrow path. Michael held his head up, glad to be outside again and feel fresh air on his skin, even though is was night-time. The man pulled aside some shrubs and there in the rocky hillside was a door whose shape was lost in the indiscernible pattern of rock.

17

The man held him while the woman opened the door with a long key. He was pulled roughly inside, his eyes catching the striking beams of the moon as it lit through the swaying tree branches the opening of the dark passage he was being pushed into. The man produced a torch and lit up the stone steps that led down into the earth. A dank, cold smell wafted up to him, shooting shivers through his body. They descended into a dark cavern which had always been cut off from the light of sun and moon, the man leading the way before him and the woman half-pushing him from behind. From far below Michael heard the dripping of water and the echoes of small stones falling. His feet had somewhat loosened the ropes round them and after he had counted ninety-four short steps they stopped and turned along a passage that itself sloped downwards. This passage seemed even darker although the light from the torch could not have so soon become dimmer. There were hanging strands of vegetation like tentacles from the roof. Their shadows moved to and fro as the torchlight played on them. At length they came to another door which they unlocked and locked again behind them.

"Where are you taking me?" Michael must have shouted out in despair. But they did not reply.

The man stepped into a corner where he lit an oil lamp that soon spread its unpleasant fumes round the poorly ventilated area. Michael was able to cast his eye round this terrifying dungeon. One corner was completely black with no light at all; there was nothing there, but from beyond came the distant sound of water and a slight draught. The area itself had two odd chairs and a rickety table. The man hung the oil lamp from a hook in the ceiling just over this table. There appeared to be a primitive fireplace set into one wall. How Michael wished for a fire now, even now in the height of summer.

The man undid the ropes round his hands and feet and bade him sit. The woman poured a cup of coffee from a flask and gave him more biscuits and a hunk of cheese.

"To keep you awake while we find out what we want to know," she explained coolly.

"Why have you brought me here? You said you'd set me free!" he pleaded bitterly.

"Eat up and be thankful," the man answered.

They sat in silence while Michael ate what he could, refusing any sort of conversation. Michael grew all the more tense and frightened while they ignored his questions and pleadings. They merely sat quite still about six feet away from him, watching every movement. At length the man spoke quietly and cruelly:

"So you're here on holiday? Do those you are staying with know what you were up to yesterday evening?"

He was trying to sound like one in authority, but the more he tried the more he sounded like one usurping it. Michael became even more convinced of the fundamentally evil intentions of the couple. He was frightened but also numbed so that his fear did not affect him as it might have done. He had the fear all right, but not the sense of danger that usually accompanies it. Perhaps it was the cold and the damp that distracted him, so that he felt the beginnings of a cold fury that these people should be treating him so. As the growing anger cleared his numbed mind, he mentally reviewed the last events, seeking a reason for the wild and obsessive concern this couple were showing for the staff. They had been after the staff and also after those to whom it belonged. But why? What use was it to them, to anyone?

The man spoke loudly, waking him from his thoughts.

"Your friends will be worried. Tell us what you have to and you will go free at once. Your uncle, is it, you're staying with? Well, he'll be so concerned by now."

"You have the staff. That's what you were after. I can tell you no more."

The man produced the staff from behind his back and raised it. Michael noticed at once that it had resumed its former shape and size.

"I have good use for this if you refuse to tell us anymore. Where is that old tramp? When and where did you last see him? Do you want to stay down here forever? Nobody would ever find you."

"How can I lead you to him if you keep me down here?"

Michael was changing his tactics. Maybe he could persuade them to lead him up to daylight again. Then his heart sank as he realized it was still night.

"So you could lead us to him? That's more like it."

"How can I lead you to him at night time?" Michael retorted, partly showing his anger. Then he added quietly:

"Perhaps you'll tell me where my uncle's bike is. I expect you've taken that too.

"Shut up!"

The man aimed a blow at him but was restrained by the woman. Clearly she had other ideas how to extract information from him.

"Look dearie, we are not cruel people. Maybe we ought to take you into our confidence. Listen. There are people, certain old folk hanging onto old things which rightfully belong to all of us, the whole country, I mean. Call them thieves if that makes it clearer. They have secrets, knowledge of ways that lead to places where great treasures lie hidden. Their way of thinking is: *damn all others. This is for us alone.* And that is how things will stay if we do nothing Now, you're not one of *them*, are you? You're one of us. So why don't you behave like it? The Welsh are an old dying nation, like old-age pensioners kept alive by our contributions. You're not one of them, are you? You know it. Their walls are crumbling and will soon bury all that they have to bequeath to us."

"What do you want from them?"

"Knowledge. Knowledge of the paths that lead to great wealth."

She opened her mouth, showing her teeth in a wide, ugly gesture that was supposed to be a smile. Her tongue moved slowly over the moisture on her lips as she repeated:

"Wealth."

"Old Owen's a poor man. He has no gold," Michael protested, outraged at such a lie.

"Don't trust these peasants who go around in rags and hide gold under their floor boards."

Then the man added:

"The gold must be dug up, exposed to the daylight, used, used to acquire things, build, increase our possessions. They leave it useless in the earth."

"We have got so far in this vault in the depths of the earth," continued the woman. "Give us the tramp and he will guide us further, to the end of our quest. Then you will see what this," and she took the staff from the man, raising it high, "this staff means and why we so sorely need it."

"Just think of that," the man muttered.

They looked at each other and smiled. At last they had convinced this youth.

"If we give you back the staff and keep close behind you, you can lure this Owen to us. We shall have him and he will not know your part in this. I think we can promise that much."

She looked at the man and he nodded approval.

The thought of betraying Old Owen immediately brought the blood flowing into Michael's head. The sheer notion of it kindled a flame in him. He stood up, clenching his fists and noticed how small the man was.

"You skunks would make me betray an old man?"

"Get back you idiot!" the man shouted, showing his blackened teeth. "I'll teach you a lesson."

The woman interposed again. She pushed Michael back calmly onto a chair and began stroking his head.

"Don't upset him," she whispered. "He means well."

Michael threw her off him but was struck hard across the face and back by the man.

"Get back onto that chair," he growled.

In pain and anger Michael sat quite still on the chair, wondering what on earth he could do. He was bleeding from the mouth and wanted to cry out through sheer misery, pain and helplessness. This dirty cheap woman was trying to trick him and the man was treating him like an animal. Nevertheless he determined that he would be the one to teach a lesson. He saw out of the corner of his eye the staff that the man had placed temporarily on the table, and as he sat hard on the chair he felt the rope that Owen had given him. It was still in his trouser pocket.

18

He stared at the uncouth couple as a hunter stares at his prey. The woman was leaning against the table and the man was moving away from it towards the oil lamp as if he were intending to unhook it and continue their journey into the depths, or even to leave Michael down here in the deep dark. He put his hand in his pocket, and this instilled new courage into him. He sensed that soon he would no more have any opportunity to help himself. The presence of the rope in his pocket and the sight of the staff on the table were goading him to action. Perhaps there was a chance, if he could surprise them and escape rapidly.

He rushed at the woman, pushing her violently over a chair as he grabbed the staff. The man spat an oath and lunged at him, but Michael attacked first, struck him with the staff over the back of the head. The man retreated, then came back at Michael who swung again at his head, missed and caught him a painful blow on the left shoulder.

"Let me out of here, you filthy dwarf!" he bellowed and the woman rushed at him shouting:

"Get him! Kick him! Kick him!" and she herself kicked at his shins. He grabbed hold of her by the clothes and threw her back onto the man who was once more coming at him. Then they both rushed together at Michael. He stepped back to get a better defensive position but found himself pinned against the wall. Within a second they would have wrested the staff from him. He was in a dark corner of the room where he saw clearly for the first time. There in the ground was a black hole, a deep hole, the entrance to a deep, deep shaft. Down this shaft Michael threw the staff and heard it clatter from side to side in its descent till he heard it no more.

"Fetch it! Fetch it!" screamed the man, black with rage. The woman's mouth was trembling like a bird's beak.

"Get it!" she squawked at him, even more hysterical than the man. She was a savage, hair all over her face, her fingers clutching at his body like someone insane.

"Get down there! Fetch it!"

They tugged him over the hole and pushed him to the ground, kicking his feet into the shaft. The man kneed him in the back and Michael's feet groped for support. He felt the rungs of an old ladder as they pushed him further and further down the shaft. The woman thrust the torch into his hand.

"Find it quickly or you'll starve to death and no one will find your body!"

They slammed down the lid of the shaft over Michael's head, and he was a prisoner in the deep dark of the underworld.

The perilous descent continued till he felt his calf muscles ache and his hands were sore from grasping and sliding down the rough ladder. Water was dripping all round him, the only sound apart from the scraping of his shoes on rung after rung. It was dripping onto his hands, shoes, shoulders and face, running incessantly down his forehead. It was the Japanese wartime torture his uncle had once described to him. Gradually the cold water seemed to be penetrating his skull and freezing him till a monumental coldness rang throughout his head. It took all his strength and determination now for him to hold onto the ladder. But he was becoming more and more unsteady; his hand slipped, then his foot and he fell. The shaft was so narrow that he banged from side to side as he fell, but thereby managed to arrest the speed of his fall. He must have fallen several feet onto a damp, half-soft surface. He touched it and shone the torch onto it. It looked very like dark moss, and to his left he noticed with relief the staff.

He shone the torch all around him. The shaft had widened out into a sort of cave. There were nooks and secluded crannies all about him. He steeled himself to the realization that very soon he would have to climb up and return to *them*. He grabbed the staff, stood up and attempted to climb the ladder. But the staff was too heavy! It was as heavy as a huge sack of grain; he simply could not ascend with it. And he could not ascend without it. He tried again but could not. He touched the ground with the end of the staff. He felt it gently pulling him forward while the rope in his pocket too seemed to be urging him on. He had to go down on his knees to follow they path they were indicating, then on his tummy like a soldier on an exercise. He was crawling into a narrow archway, barely one foot high. He moved into it and with the staff pushed aside a lump of rock. The torch lit up a tunnel ahead, a tunnel for an animal, for a fox stealing away from the hounds and the staff urged him along it.

He could just crawl along, shuffling his hips, left forward, right forward, clasping the staff in one hand and the torch in the other. Every now and then he stopped to shine the torch directly in front of him. He saw no end to the tunnel and the cold was now invading his body. Only movement saved him from reaching that state of ultimate cold when all life begins to fade. And it was impossible to go back; he could neither turn round nor go backwards. He longed to fall sleep and wake up in a warm comfortable bed. He banged the crown of his head on some hard piece of rock. That brought him back to reality. Surely now the tunnel was becoming so narrow that further progress would be impossible.

Despair was about to conquer him decisively as it grew hard to breathe adequately, when the tunnel barely perceptibly broadened and warmer air seemed to be wafting into his face. He regained a little energy and grew excited as a glimmer of hope filtered into his consciousness. The staff was pulling him faster like an impatient dog on a lead. There was definitely more room in the tunnel now; his going was easier but he could not stop to rest; the staff did not allow him to do so.

It was as though he was creeping towards the centre of an underground nest. The tunnel was now gradually descending deeper and the air, such as it was, was warmer, pleasant or even, incredibly, fresher. He was moving deeper into the earth: farther and farther away from all things he knew. But it was not like a descent into the bowels of the earth: it was more like progress towards a point he knew or at least the staff knew. The going now was comparatively easy except for wisps of down irritating his nostrils.

The tunnel was now much larger; he could crawl on his knees and get along faster. The staff pulled like a piston and rod on a steam locomotive. Now he was excited that he might indeed find a way out of his predicament. Then all of a sudden the tunnel came to an end. He slipped through a hole and fell safely onto a bed of down. He was on a huge nest made up of enormous feathers. A time ago in the distant past this must have been the nest of a huge bird. He lay down gasping the fresher air and within a few seconds was asleep.

After an unrecorded length of time he was awake, took the torch and examined the dome-shaped vault into which he had emerged. The roof was not unlike that of the cave above into which that man and woman had dragged him. But here the only feasible entrance was through the roof and how could he possibly get up there, eight or nine feet? The light of the torch was getting dimmer and reminded Michael forcibly of his situation, trapped in the middle of the earth. He felt the staff and the thought woefully crossed his mind that it might be some evil agent leading him to perdition. Perhaps, perhaps after all the couple up there had been right and had been really trying to help him. Now he had refused their help and was here alone. He put down the staff and stood up and examined the walls to see if there were, after all, any chance of climbing up to the hole in the roof, but he found none.

He sat down again and looked for the staff. He could not find it. He scoured all parts of the nest in the fading light but it had apparently vanished. Where could it have gone? It might have sunk through the soft layer of feathers. He groped down amongst them, but in vain.

Then the horror of his situation took hold of him: he was going to die, not immediately, not for sometime perhaps, but he would die here, cut off from his uncle, his family and those he had got to know on his holiday. What was his uncle doing now? What was the lovely Victoria doing? She was in her garden perhaps – anyway she was in the open air the sky over her, her fine blue eyes flashing in the sunlight and the wind in her hair. How he wished he had told her how much he liked her! Now he knew it was too late. And on top of this he realized the pain he had caused his uncle – he would die without being able to apologize to him, unreconciled with those he had quarrelled with, die with nothing to show for his life, merely a young eighteen-year-old who had disappeared never to be seen again.

He sat unmoving and tried to repress his tears – no need, for there was no one to witness him weeping. He might as well weep then, only no tears came. The emotion was dammed, welled up inside.

He started to move about restlessly, frustrated that he could not give vent to the emotion within. He shifted around on the huge nest and underneath him the feathers moved up and down in waves. He ceased moving but the movement beneath him carried on. He moved back: the feathers like waves on the sea billowed up and fell about him. There was something alive beneath.

He pulled away at the centre, throwing them off into a pile in a corner, but the movement continued from even further below. He tunnelled lower and lower, shining every now and then the dim torch at his feet. Then he saw the top of the staff moving persistently up and down. It was banging away at something solid beneath. He grabbed more feathers and dug carefully deeper, flinging the feathers away from him. Eventually he had moved all the feathers from this one area and came to a thin bed of straw, uncovering the full length of the staff. It was hammering of its own accord against wood. He pulled back the straw and at his feet he uncovered an old, extremely old trapdoor. On it were inscribed letters in a strange tongue:

Y gwreiddyn cul ydyw'r gwaelod byd llidiart byd.

19

He took hold of the ring in the trap door and pulled at it. It would not budge. He tried again and again but was not able to move it even the tiniest fraction of an inch. He hit it with the staff to try to break it in, but it proved as firm as a rock and moreover he hurt his hands by using the staff in this way.

A gentle pressure guided his hand to his trouser pocket where the rope was. He pulled it out and automatically tied it round his waist. His vision grew blurred and all swam indistinctly before him. He rubbed his eyes but his blurred vision remained. It was as if he needed glasses like his sister. He sought to untie the knot in the rope but he could not find it. Then he laid aside the torch and took hold of the staff with both hands. An outside force seemed to be guiding him. At once his vision cleared, and he saw brightly and clearly around him and onto the door at his feet. And now those words were intelligible to him:

The root of the narrow is the bottom of the world
the gate of the world

It was like a riddle he had heard as a child. Was it challenging him to unravel its meaning? Was this then the bottom of the world? And if so, how could it be a gate? Would it open? He tugged once more at the ring on the trap door and this time it opened. He fell over backwards at the abrupt opening and stared through the gap, the escape hatch suddenly was revealed to him. Slowly memories of old days past climbed up through the hole into his head. He was a tiny child, helpless in bed, waiting for his mother to come, waiting on the food that was due to him. He recalled that one particular day when it had occurred, that he was able with great effort to turn his head to face the window. Then the light had streamed in on him so strongly that he would have shielded his eyes had his soft baby hands been capable of such movement. From outside, as though it was an enormous wave of water, the light inundated him as a beam of sunlight shot through the glass. But he had not needed to shield his eyes. The shielding came from outside, from the trees. Those light green leaves in their wonderful soothsome shapes were carefully protecting him from the full power of the light, that he might enjoy it, and the patterns it created and the colours, that the light which showed him all should not blind him from all. Now he was able to turn away his head without difficulty and observe the dances of those patterns and the gentle spring colours on the wall, and the interplay of shadow and light on the shiny door. And just as easily he was able to turn his head back to the direct light, and laugh and chuckle at the extreme sensation of joy that the world could respond to his endeavours, and that he had as it were climbed up a further step in his young life.

And as through that window long ago, light, warm golden light and gentle breezes streamed upwards through the hole that Michael had opened on this day; he had regained his feet and was climbing through it, staff and torch in his hand and the rope round his waist. He alighted on a slab of stone. He was standing at the top of a long flight of steps, looking down into an immense hall that was illuminated by this golden light and enlivened by the breeze. This was the other side of the gate: a great expanse after the narrowness of the tunnel!

He went down a few steps that he might have a fuller view of where he was. He was at the far back of the hall which stretched for some hundred and fifty to two hundred feet before him. The roof was a gentle arch, a short arc from an enormous circle. The whole hall was lit by numerous golden lights, concealed along the top of, and halfway down, the longer walls. At the other end of the hall a large area of the floor was raised about two feet higher to form a platform, though the platform was like the rest of the floor, solid rock.

In the corner, directly opposed to that from which Michael surveyed this vastness, was a passage, similarly arched, leading off. He could just about make out the flicker of less intense lights filtering through from this passage.

As his eyes grew more accustomed to the scene in front of him, he was able to discern the colours on the roof above him: triangles and rectangles of reds and blues, greens and gold, interlocking figures throwing back the light that was cast on them, throwing back a light fuller, transformed by diverse colour. Similar patterns adorned the two longer walls, while the one at the end gave forth multitudes of opulent but sober colours all radiating from one huge, sky-blue circle in its centre. The floor was delicately glazed granite, making it hard to comprehend whether the hues and shades were its own or merely reflections of the splendour above and around it. The platform was lustreless and void of colour, but at its centre, some two yards from the wall rose the majestic seat, surely a throne, a seat fit for kings.

Yet as Michael stared at the wonder before him, and in awe descended the steps his heart was sad: had he come then too late with his trust? Was the glory past that had been vaunted here and had spread further abroad, upwards to upper earth and air? Was he the young man who had arrived too late for the feast, when the guests had gone and only the decorations remained? For the first time in his life he felt that sadness which all feel at one time when time passes away and the glory with it: the great buildings fall, and trees and vast forests are felled or burnt down, and people too – our fathers, mothers and companies of great men and warriors collapse, flee or die. What is left are merely memories and echoes of great times.

Yet some believe they will return, given patience and the will. Michael no longer knew whether it was him clasping the staff or the staff that was controlling him. Although it made him restless and urged him to move on, it also, by some paradox of feeling, urged him to stay here, for here was the end, the goal they had been striving towards. So now another feeling intruded on the sense of the past that had at first possessed him: that this was where he had to remain until the blurred vision of his destiny had cleared.

He held the staff aloft – or rather, it guided his hand as if reaching for the roof in order to point something out. Michael was now more or less in the centre of the hall and glanced upward to take in the amazing vastness of this structure. He now saw clearly these glorious shapes, colours, patterns beaming down on him in their reflected light. And through all the roof, as he contemplated it it, he saw, penetrating and displaying themselves, the tentacles of an enormous root, and at this root the staff pointed, as towards a kindred source. The staff was showing him the entire vaulted roof of the hall, the hall at the root of the world!

He stood for moments, looking and absorbing wordlessly. Slowly, however, he grew tired and conscious of the weakness of his body, the trials and straits it had been through. His mind was asking once more how he could escape to the world he knew, where there was food and drink to fill his stomach and people whom he loved to be with. He looked again at the passage leading off, the passage on the left that led into the hall. He felt on his face the fresh scented air that came along it and was impelled towards it. This was his only hope and he walked directly towards it, bearing the staff with him. He walked into the archway and switched the weak torchlight on again to grope along the slowly upward-winding passage. The alluring scent grew more intense as he strode forward, and a light, at first dim, became stronger, as did the tramping sound of many feet that were approaching. The voices, voices echoing, chanting, conversing in queer rhythms wafted like the scent around him. Michael turned to run back across the hall and up the steps. He took refuge at the top. There was no escape.

20

The tramp, tramp, tramp of many feet, and the steady increase in the light, as though the hall were lighting up in welcome, all this struck him with instant fear of being discovered in this foreign place. The reverberation of the oncoming feet resounded round the hall into his body, a series of oscillations that crossed the shivers that beset him.

He crouched as still as he was able in the half-shadows that fell across the top of the steps, resting the staff on the steps immediately below him. He felt uneasy where he was but could not determine the reason. Was it that he had been unable to escape back up through the trapdoor, or that he felt guilty at having run away from those approaching? Perhaps he would remain unseen up here and be able to slip out along the passage after they had gone. After all they must be coming from somewhere outside and he had the rope to hide him as it had done before, from his enemies. But maybe these new arrivals were not his enemies.

He huddled at the top of the steps, waiting and trembling as the steps grew near. He felt cold again in his anxiety, as he tried to wrap what thin summer clothing he was wearing more tightly round him. Now the sound of the tramping feet was very loud indeed; the individual paces became clearer and the gleam from the arriving torches spread further into the hall, leaving little unaffected by the increasing light. It was the approach of fire: two rows of flaming torches emerged out of the passage into the hall, illuminating the area as if for a ceremonial banquet. The files of torch-bearers divided and took up positions around the perimeter. Quite still these figures stood, obscured by the lights they held above themselves.

A slower moving, more dignified procession now entered, flanked by bearers of gentler, warmer lights with steadier flames. This was surely the core of the procession.

Michael was still cowering up there, a frightened stray animal before those who would soon find him out, judge and sentence him. His eyes watered as he regarded the assembled company.

The torches round the edge of the hall burned brighter, more intensely, illuminating the deep gold that was the predominating colour, glowing up there on the roof between those gigantic tree roots, roots that must have taken centuries to spread, to raise the trunk and to have grown, grown through rock and soil, and ages long after other trees had grown, been felled while new trees were planted. What struck him was not just the richness of the scene but its fine, resplendent beauty. Here on this roof was the light that lit the underworld, the beauty nourishing the earth in times of darkness outside, preserving till the time to surface came and the sunlight took up the hidden treasure. This was no wealth to mine for, to hack at and cart away. It was a heritage to be tended by the few till the few became the many.

But there was no further time to brood. Four stately figures clad in pure white robes were entering the hall. Side by side they strode, maidens holding erect candelabra, seven candles each held aloft and shining out. They approached the platform and took up posts at its four corners. There followed one in white with flowing black hair, bearing tilted in front of her a huge round golden dish from which the light streamed forth as from the sun. Then came two men in multi-coloured garments, as heralds, carrying each a long polished trumpet, and behind them one more maiden dressed in rich blue velvet, the sky from which the sun shone, her long blond hair streaming over her shoulders. She held a golden chalice, glinting with rubies that must certainly dazzle all by their radiance, and behind an aged man, staggering, helped along by two knights on foot. The crown weighed heavy on the old man's head. At the rear a young knight on horseback, proudly erect on his frisky white steed. He was the last in this weird procession.

All these last took up position on the stone platform as the king was helped to his granite throne. The blue-clad maiden stood at his right hand, the glinting light of the stones in his crown and on the chalice played together, adding blue and red and green to the golden light of the dish, which the maiden held calmly as she stood her place, on the left hand of the king.

The trumpeters on either side of the platform raised their instruments and peals of sounds cut like a sword through the now still air. Michael was sure he would not be noticed in such an auspicious gathering.

The company of torch-bearers left their positions against the walls and formed two semicircles facing the throne. Gradually they broke one by one into song, the singing of a choir, sad, in mourning – slow and unworldly harmonies, a lament in softly rising tones that all there took up till the music filled the hall. The walls seemed to expand, the music was penetrating the earth to the roots of the tree, transmitted beyond these walls, rising up through the earth to sky, where men and animals might hear it, rising and pleading to be heard amongst all the other sounds up there, where Michael now so longed to be.

He sat and listened, caught up by the melody: this song he knew – the song he had so faintly heard from far away beneath the Four Kings' Stones. He knew now the need within him to help, to give something that he might still the lament and the cause for grief; it was an urge that pulled him down to them if he did not resist.

Now movement was replacing song: the maiden moved towards the king and lowered the chalice; the knights on either side raised him that his lips might reach the rim. But before his lips could touch it he sank back in his throne, his head hung low and arms limp at his side. He raised his head an inch and with a feeble gesture motioned her away. He was unequal to the ordeal. The maiden resumed her former position, her head bent in grief.

The young knight on horseback rode in front of the platform and addressed them. The king raised his head and muttered a reply, and a general murmuring began amongst those on the platform. The maid in white put down the golden dish and approached the king to wipe his brow. All turned to face the king and the lament began again. The sound flooded the hall and flowed along the roof, as if an underground river of sound had broken loose and was gradually seeping in. The lament subsided and once more the maiden approached the king with the chalice. This time he took of it. At first it seemed that he had now the strength to raise himself and address them all, but at the last moment his strength failed him. He sank back on his throne and all looked upon him with compassion. The young knight on the horse drew back and the maiden, on a sign from the king, moved with the chalice to the edge of the platform, raising it aloft to the whole assembled company.

It was as though the central point of some ceremony had been reached and then halted as its continuation faltered. For all stood silent and did not approach the cup; the unnatural pause was confusing them. The young knight rode forward to the middle of the hall and called out an appeal, a cry that echoed away down the long darkened passage and up to Michael where he was crouching. A second time the knight called out. He stood up high in the saddle; the horse pawed the ground restlessly, interrupting the silence with hoof-beats. For a third time the knight called out:

"Let the fool come forward with the spear! Let him come forward!"

This time Michael understood what was required of him and beheld surprised a spear in his hand, the spear that he had been bearing in its secret mutation, the property of those down there, of the king who dwelt beneath the earth. And it was not being forced from him; he was surrendering it of his own freewill.

He had at last understood. In his hand he held the shining, gleaming, upright spear. He was guided in a half-trance down the steps. All stood in silence, awaiting him as he descended and made his way past the ranks towards the royal platform. He was moving towards the maiden, slowly towards the king, shyly as one approaches for the first time such a presence. He scarcely durst make a sound, so softly did he tread. He trembled as he held the spear. It pulled him forward in his final task to deliver it to its owners, after years of lease – safe and returned to glory. As it pulled him further he knew he had the confidence he needed to reach the platform's edge.

He walked past the knight; the maiden clad in blue came near to meet him. The light from the chalice lit up his eyes and warmed his body. She held out the chalice to him.

"Drink," she whispered to him.

Michael put his lips to the rim, which she tilted kindly to make drinking easier. He drank. A life glowed and shone in him as the summer sun had so often done in the open landscape: a richness of light, a beauty, a glow of colour and a body that was flesh and earth and sky entered him with a soft liquid balm. He looked at her, at her eyes, and earth and sky were there as well, in the lakes of her eyes so blue and deep they showed the firmament. He looked deep below their surface and felt that all shone within them. In her the shapes, till now but tangled patterns, shapes of a jigsaw, fitted together and became a whole – the tangle of events that had led him here assumed a straight, inevitable line – the fresh sunlit countryside and the mists of reddening evening, the journey down the tunnel, the descent along the almost impenetrable passage to the nest of down, the gate at the bottom of the world and on through the root at the narrowest point – urged on by the staff to this, to this one moment.

He beheld her fine blond hair cascading over her shoulders, a cascading stream over her garments, he beheld her body as it breathed alive and present in front of him.

"Take this," he uttered quietly, "I believe it's yours."

She placed the chalice in another's hands and took the spear. Her hand touched his and he stretched out his right hand to stroke her hair, the living sheaves of his eyes' food. He had his proof that she was real. She stepped back to show the king the spear.

Michael looked at the company around him and sensed the joy the spear had brought them. He looked once more at the decorated floor and the lofty roof between the roots of that great tree. The weapon had reached its home, whither the carvings on it in the end had guided it. The knight rode up to him.

"You have brought it to us at last. Long we have waited. Once more the spear is safe among us. We thought you lost and lacking patience and the will. But time and nature worked together for a good end. The spear has guided slowly all the way; now await full growth."

His words flowed softly as brooks flow through meadows, where there is no other noise – as water flowing, smoothing with time all those jagged rocks that vast destructive upheavals had rendered sharp and dangerous. Michael looked at him and recognized Old Owen young.

The knight spoke on:

"You have given and received. Take now what you have and remember us. I shall guide you upwards to the sky. You have the strength to go that distance. Remember us. You have seen what lies beneath the people of this ancient land, a people driven by conquest and others' greed to the sea's edge and to these subterranean halls. We leave behind us pillage, devastation and a broken tongue. Remember us and strive to keep the vision. Pray help that light to shine."

Michael drank these words, even as the chalice had replenished him and gazed once more at her in the blue garment. He caught those warm lake eyes as the lights from many torches and the reflected light from the dish and chalice rose to overcome him in brightness. The chalice inflicted the more penetrating glow.

She was there before him as he left, his own soul's reflection.

A strong arm lifted him onto the horse and they moved away from the light. He was travelling along that passageway with the knight. A new triumphant song struck up in the hall as they left. These last moments flashed in his mind's eye as they journeyed upwards. His body sang with them. He clutched the pommel to steady himself. He swayed but did not fall as that blinding vision threatened to dash him to the rocky floor against which the horse's hooves rhythmically echoed.

"Hold tight," the voice with him said, "the journey up is uneven, but if you will you have the strength."

21

The horse clumped slowly upwards, Michael's arms clasping the body of the knight, his hands gripping his tunic. Fatigue was now taking hold of him; yet he also felt strong from the encounter down there and a new determination to hold on, to survive with these riches on which his eyes had feasted. He saw nothing but the vague image of the body of the knight moving sturdy and erect immediately before him. Neither was his mind clear: just a series of blurred images, one replacing the other, then blending with it, images now indistinct after what had been clear and balanced.

"You have seen so much," the knight told him in a low voice. "Never forget it, whatever comes across your life and tries to obscure it. Hold on to it. Many let it go, and with it the deep trust of our ancient people. Furthermore, the richness that you have seen down there will be yours, transformed into your normal life, for you have learnt to feel and know some of the depths which feeling may stir up."

The ascent had become rougher. The steed stumbled over uneven stones and many times they bent their heads or leaned to one side as their headroom diminished. Sometimes they waded through underground streams or stumbled over fallen rocks. Once they encountered the crumbled trunk of an old tree, almost broken off from its roots.

"Once a time ago the light came as far as here," the knight told him.

The old tree was quite withered, a hawthorn with crooked broken branches. At its roots a tiny stream of water trickled. They stopped a while as they guided themselves carefully round it. The horse's hooves pushed some earth into the opening of the spring.

They now reached a very narrow section where Michael doubted whether they could pass: surely not even one man could force his way through. A huge tree-root emerged from the soil and rock blocked their path. But the knight rode confidently on and they got past.

"Part of the root of that great tree which holds aloft our present world," he remarked. "Few penetrate this far from above and have the courage to pass this point."

"But how can they? How can they get through the narrow opening?" Michael asked.

"They must stretch themselves to gain a footing through. Few are willing to be stretched. Hold fast."

Michael clasped on tightly as he felt his grip relaxing. The breeze was now a strong wind and they smelt the sunlit air coming down to greet them. They passed recesses in the rock. Bones were scattered here and there on the floor.

"The bones of those who ventured up and lost the way down again, or sometimes those of our enemies who sought to smoke us out but could not stretch themselves through the gap."

"But I did not come this way; I was led another," Michael exclaimed, more alert now from the freshness of the air.

"That was a dangerous threat to us, that those who imprisoned you should find another way. Our good fortune that you kept hold of the staff and rope and had the courage."

"But would they ever have found their way along the narrow passage and the door at the very end?"

"Who knows what they might have done had they had the staff. But now that is passed. We have it again, and you who brought it will remember these events as you live on in the sunlight. Once every several generations the staff must go above so that we have a presence in the world till our time comes."

The rush of air and water and living tendrils shooting from the great deep root were now dominating the passage as it quickly widened. Daylight was seeping through some of the cracks. The water from the surface soil was dripping onto Michael's forehead, a cool and refreshing touch. And the smell of air-soaked earth renewed him as it touched his nostrils.

"We are near the top and soon must part. Remember us as we are and not as you see us above. Up here I am an old man weary and slow of step, a creature without nobility."

He turned on his saddle now that the way was more open and freer and looked at Michael as if to take from him a promise. Michael looked once more into the young blue eyes of Old Owen as he had been, as he was now.

"Keep to the vision if you can."

"But if I forget or become confused, or simply cannot remember clearly?"

"You have many years, and the purity of what you have seen cannot remain. What can remain, however, is your faith that something of another world still lives, that where and how you live is not the only way, that full life goes beyond your walls and reaches us. Do not give up. Act out your life with the knowledge of its breadth."

The roots of trees and grasses brushed and soiled their faces, and the path drew to its steepest as it widened further. Finally the way came to its close, to open onto grounds Michael knew. He closed his eyes at the onrush of light, and at the final moment a vision of the beautiful maiden came once more to him before it too faded as he trod the open ground.

"Now the staff can again be with us. The earth is once more in balance and will not sway from its course. And as when all balances are restored it will rock at times, cause even perceptible reverberations – but this shows a more stable time is near."

And as he spoke the horseman raised himself in his stirrups to take in the abundant air. The air had come upon them as if a dam had been breached; they both bent back under the power of the unleashed stream as they climbed further up the hill out of the shadow into the full sunlight. Michael shielding his eyes crouched low behind the back of the knight who took the sun full in the face. Michael's eyes, so dazzled, lost their power of focus as they felt the freedom of the open spaces around them.

The mists before his eyes – were they real or only within him? Once more the vision of the beautiful maiden was there before him projected onto a vaporous screen. Once more it vanished, and he dismounted and prepared to go further alone on foot.

"Here we must part. What you have been through will be a memory. If we meet again it will be on a different plane. Take the rope from around you when you are safe and burn it. We shall catch the ashes."

At these words he turned and raised his hand in farewell. Michael took one look behind him as the horseman disappeared into the white mist coming from the passage. He heard the clump of the hooves on stone, then the sound too was gone. He set out clear of the mists. The sun beat down heavy on him, and he felt the weight of the rucksack he had carried without noticing all this while. He felt inside and found a crumpled biscuit. He was hungry and he ate it. He walked buoyantly down the hill, stooping over a fast running stream to catch a handful of water. He was under a small group of birch trees. He looked up and beheld in joy the leaves filtering the sunlight, all patterns, designs thrown up by the earth to hold the sky.

His half-dreamy state left him as the cold water rushed through his fingers. He knew he had to get back to his uncle's. How worried he would have been about him! He had no idea how long he had been absent. He looked round the land about him, recognizing its shape and then the direction in which he must go. He became aware that even though he had handed over the staff, yet it was somehow still with him. Then he remembered the bicycle. He found the shed and the bike inside, mounted and rode back the way he had come before, oblivious as to whether he might be seen. He cycled past the Kings' Stones and down the lane towards his uncle's house.

The sun beat on his back, neck and shoulders as he pedalled slowly towards the path that would take him to the house by the back. He struggled tired with the bike along the path, through the gate into the back garden.

22

The garden appeared different to him now: a familiar place, as the house itself was, but it was different. Knowledge of what lay beneath rendered it fuller, gave it deeper roots and a significance he had missed before.

He hardly had time to place the bike against the wall before Kate rushed out of the kitchen to accost him. Where had he been? They had been so worried: two nights and the best part of two days out and not a word to them. Of course they had had to inform the police. What had happened to him? He looked all right – Why then had he been away so long?

Michael tried to calm her by avoiding direct answers and asking for his uncle. He was told to go upstairs and see him. He climbed the stairs anxiously, wondering how much to tell and how to tell it. The reality of what had happened to him now beset him as something even beyond the fantasy of those with a deal of imagination. The whole weight of his experience was pressing hard on him. He felt too in one corner of his mind a reluctance that he should have to betray this so secret chapter in his life, even to his understanding uncle. Yet he could not avoid it. He knocked and walked slowly into his uncle's study.

"Hello Uncle Hugh." He tried to smile, but under the force of the midday heat he was suddenly overcome with fatigue. He flopped onto the sofa and half closed his eyes.

"I'm sorry; I'm so tired. I was taken away and have only just got free."

"Who was it? How did this happen?"

His uncle got up and came over to him, shaking him gently by the shoulder.

"That man and woman, they did it. They are horrible people."

He was fast asleep. His uncle tried to pick him up, but he was too heavy. He dragged him to his bedroom and pulled him onto his bed, removing his shoes and laying a light blanket over him.

Michael slept for about eighteen hours, a sleep undisturbed by any dreams he could remember and disturbed by only a short period of wakefulness in the middle of the night, when he awoke cold, leaned out of the window to the starlit night, undressed and climbed into the bed itself to fall into a deeper sleep.

He awoke with the sun beating in onto his face through the open window. He dozed for a while, in the hope that some dream might bring back all the wonderful things he had experienced during the past hours. But his mind was not capable of it, neither was his stomach for he was naturally extremely hungry. He washed and dressed. He went warily downstairs to see what he could find to eat.

He met his uncle as soon as he stepped into the hall. He had been waiting for him in the drawing room. He motioned him in there and pointed to a tray of food and a flask of coffee that had been prepared for him. Michael sat down and ate, silently. His uncle spoke no word to him. When Michael had finished he thanked his uncle. His mind was totally blank; there were simply no thoughts in it. Despite the hot day he did not feel warm. He was incapable of reacting to heat or cold.

"Had enough?" Uncle Hugh asked.

"Yes thank you."

His uncle took the tray away and as he left the room he remarked:

"I've told the police you've come back and are safe. Of course they'll have to come and ask you questions, particularly as you say you were kidnapped. Stay here please till I come back."

Michael heard him put the tray down in the kitchen and speak a few words to Kate. Then he was back, sitting facing Michael as before.

"I guessed that your disappearance had something to do with those people who had been pestering you. Was I right?"

"Yes. They were after that old shepherd's staff. They tried to take it from me. They shut me up for hours but I escaped."

"Where do they live? Any idea?"

Michael told him exactly where the house was and his uncle said he would inform the police. These people must be identified. He told Michael that they had held onto the dog until their suspicions had been confirmed or discounted.

"And why did they want the staff?" He looked at him intently, lowering his voice. "Do you know why they were after it?"

There was a glint in his uncle's eye as if he knew at least half the answer.

"How did you find the courage to stand up to those kidnappers?"

Michael replied that their insistence had increased his obstinacy.

"Somehow I found the courage when they made me angry."

Michael explained as he thought best that they attached an almost superstitious value to it. He was uncertain as to how far his uncle accepted his story.

"Maybe they are dangerous cranks," was all Uncle Hugh would comment.

His uncle leant back in his armchair and was silent for a while. He did know something about the staff and that it was supposed to possess some secret quality. He recalled having seen it when he last stayed with Michael's parents and had wondered then that it rested so apparently neglected against a wall in their living room. Yes, Uncle Joe had held it as a trust, as he had once put it. He wondered aloud what exactly this trust had been.

Now Michael explained triumphantly how he had been able to hand it back. He did not mention Old Owen, but told him instead how he had handed it over to an old shepherd he had met 'in the hills', an old shepherd who had recognized it and told of its value to his generations.

He sensed that his uncle understood, although he possibly did not interpret 'in the hills' in the way Michael had meant it. Uncle Hugh stood up and went into the hall to telephone the police. They would be coming round later in the day for details, and they would in the meantime keep an eye on the house Michael had indicated.

The police arrived later in the evening. Michael had been asked not to leave the premises till they had spoken to him, lest those people try to recapture him. He had spent a boring and hot afternoon talking to Jack and reading. But his mind was far from clear enough to concentrate for long, as his thoughts flitted from the time of his imprisonment to that wonderful vision of the other world he had visited in the hills.

The police informed him that the house Michael had described had been vacated, probably within the last twenty-four hours. They had looked through all the windows and there was no sign of life inside. The garage too had been empty. All they recounted was that two large crows perched on the apex of the roof had flown down aggressively at them as they had been staring through the windows. None of the inhabitants of the houses nearby had known the occupants who had kept very much to themselves.

Michael then had to describe as clearly as possible the man and woman. He dwelt longer on the description of the woman – her flamboyant, painted and cheaply groomed appearance, the ingratiating way she had handled him. The man he passed off as an ill-tempered little bully. The police congratulated him on his successful escape and undertook to alert all local forces to keep a lookout for his abductors and their black car.

He was still very tired and retired early to bed that night. His dazed mind still throbbed with the many events that had crowded these last days. As he lay there his wandering fantasies changed from the figure of the wild, scheming woman, to her likewise without a name, who had stood there before him, her hair flowing over her fine garments and her wonderfully blue eyes shining into him as she had given him the chalice, to drink that warm and soothing liquid.

23

For the second night in succession his sleep was deep and long. He woke this time feeling fully refreshed after his strenuous adventures; at ease too, and more or less confident that his uncle bore him no ill will for the concern he had caused. He was sure that his account of the events had been accepted; indeed it was certainly corroborated by the sudden abandoning by the man and woman of the house they had occupied near the Harley Valley.

He felt now more at ease; a peace had settled in him. He had gained strength and insight into the world about him. It was a peace that brought him closer to the wonderful intimate landscape he was in: the hills, soft meadows and rugged stones, the ancient pathways that led to half-open secrets of their past, but not in words, merely in the patterns they made as they traversed the countryside. He was closer to the people here too, to his uncle and to others ...

He rose in the continuing summer warmth and looked out over the intricate network of fields and hills and the paths of men and animals which criss-crossed them, making them appear noble attempts to order land against the primitive background of tracks and stone markings. He raised his eyes and gazed in the direction of Bach Hill and behind it Hergest Ridge. Did he still hear the singing of that assembly or was it alive now in his memory only, as his vision of her was? He was happier than before, but the renewed strength in his limbs stirred and gnawed at him to undertake something more. There was yet much to be found.

Michael dressed hurriedly and bounded into the breakfast room, wishing a warm good morning to all there. Kate poured him his tea. He looked at her weather-torn hands as they poured so carefully. He tried to imagine how these hands had been when they were young and was moved to see they were now as delicate as ever; only their surface had been touched by age, by the wrinkles and dryness that sets in as hands attain their age when the work they perform is more important than the pleasure they give when youthful. He looked at her face and believed he saw her as when young. Then a flash, and she was old again as here now. He saw her as one grown as one with the house and its surroundings, someone with a share in the air here.

"How long have you lived here?" he asked her.

"Well all my life I've lived here, Michael, and my father too, when the old master Mr John lived here with his large family. My father's father lived down the road. See! You know the old clump of trees where the cottage was? He lived and died there, and my father, and for a short time his brother, were up here in the service of Mr John. And Victoria's family have been here too for some generations. Have you been to see her since your return?"

Michel, embarrassed, chose not to answer. He certainly was keen to see her, but in his own time. There were things he wanted to sort out beforehand.

"So you know this area well?" Michael continued inquisitively. "Do you know anything of the legends or old stories of these parts?"

"Some that I heard from my father. They say the Welsh tribes were driven here after losing their last great battle – just a few managed to get here with their king. Some folk say they are hiding and wait to return."

He listened as Kate recounted the stories that haunted the area, where she had always lived. Her voice seemed to take on the reverberations and invisible patterns or rhythms that he felt in the air, as she told him of field and hedgerow stained with blood and of secret signs left by those hiding under the stones and in the copses. She spoke of tracks now overgrown which one might go along, if one found them, and be transported into bygone ages.

Beyond her face the country outside, the trees, fields and tracks, all were as witnesses to what she was relating, to that hidden world that still grew unobserved around them. The sun shone onto her white hair, and he got up and went into the garden to see if his uncle were there. He walked down the path by the kitchen door and saw Jack by the shed. He was tidying up the pots and plants straggling from rapid growth in this hot, humid summer. Like Kate he was part of this house and its grounds. His supple ageing body moved and involved itself with the plants as if he were one with soil, garden and everything here.

"Morning Michael," Jack called over his shoulder. "Looking for your uncle? He came out and went straightaway back upstairs."

Michael thanked him and strolled under the birch trees to the end of the garden. He leant on the gate and stared at the hill in front of him. It was not as high as the hills the other side of the house, but the late morning sun was lighting up the yellows and the scorched greens. It shone onto the few scattered rocks, onto the almost non-reflecting stone. Higher up on the near horizon stood the few scraggy trees of this hill, skeletons against the sky. Two large crows flew restlessly from one tree to another in ever widening curves.

Michael pulled at the tall grass in the field beside him, thinking it was time for a hay harvest. He thoughtlessly twisted the stalks round his fingers, dropped them down onto the ground and set off dreamily back to the house, up the stairs and to his uncle's room. He wondered whether to knock but his uncle opened the door and invited him in. He had heard the floor creaking outside and had guessed Michael was there.

His uncle did not look well; he looked troubled and his face was strained, tensely knit and more wrinkled. He offered Michael a chair and started to tell him about his work.

"I've come to a point I can't get beyond: one of the most unforgettable days with Alice up in the hills above Rhayader. We went walking, walked for hours in the hope of passing right over the hills and dropping down near an old ruined abbey so far from all later civilization. A spirit from old times seems always present there. One can stand there and look back at the hills one has just walked across and wonder at the transformation of the landscape: it is as though one is back in an ancient era. Anyway, we managed that long hike and promised ourselves that we should one day return and do it again. The walk we never managed again. We had to turn back, you see, but I cannot remember why. I just cannot remember and it's an important part of my life. It was something I should not forget, but I have."

He ran his hand through his sparse hair and slapped his hand down on the desk.

"Here, have a sip of beer." He offered Michael a small glassful. Michael raised the glass and drank.

"Here's to your memory, Uncle Hugh. Perhaps you'd remember better if you took a short break outside in the fresh air."

"It's not my memory. No, I don't think it's that. I don't think I knew what sent us back. We set out, well equipped, but simply turned back after a time."

He put down his pen and stood up.

"You're right. I must get outside and the fresh air should help me to sort things out. Perhaps we could go over to Rhayader together. How about the day after tomorrow? That would give me time to get a few things together."

Michael was delighted at this suggestion. He valued the time his uncle was prepared to give him. Going over to Rhayader and walking with him across the mountains, that was indeed an exciting prospect! He wasn't due back home for a short time yet and was not able to think of a better way to fill that time than with Uncle Hugh whom he had grown so fond of. Of course, he at once said he would love to accompany him and offered to help in any way he could. Uncle Hugh suggested he might sort out the relevant maps that were all in his study.

This Michael did in no time. He placed them on the study room table as his uncle had requested and then went out into the garden. He chatted once more with Jack before deciding to take a stroll down the path at the back of the house. The wind had got up but it was still fairly sunny. Occasionally a few high clouds cut out the direct sunlight, but they soon passed and the sharp shadows reappeared along the path.

He was pleasantly surprised to meet Victoria coming towards him; she was taking a dog for a walk. The frisky dog bounded up to him wagging its tail as if it recognized him. Victoria came up close behind it, recognizing Michael at once, smiling and greeting him.

"Where did you get to then?" were her first words. "We heard you were missing and were worried something had happened to you."

24

She was close to him now. Michael looked into her bright eyes and smiled back at her.

"I was OK," he answered. "Just a couple of idiots who tried to kidnap me."

"Kidnap you?" she looked at him earnestly and at that moment some of the shine went from her eyes as a shadow crossed her face.

Michael looked up as he heard the flutter of wings close above them. It was two black crows again.

"They are mistaking us for prey," he muttered.

"I hope they are mistaking us. I don't like them. Not all the birds in these parts are nice. But you are back and seem all right. That must have been nasty, when you were kidnapped, I mean. Were you very scared."

"At first, but then they made me so angry I struck out and escaped. I hid in a shed in the hills where I spent the night. Now the police are on their track."

"Why do you think they kidnapped you?" She was curious to know.

"Can I tell you later?" he asked; he was not sure how he could put over his almost unbelievable adventure.

"All right then," she replied, not entirely satisfied with his answer.

Nevertheless she took the hint and continued:

"You like exploring the hills, don't you? I love it too. I sometimes go up into the hills near here. I love wandering about and exploring as you do, but I always take Nick with me. That's my dog."

Michael replied that he was pleased she liked that too, but was a little too nervous to suggest they went out together.

She began then to tell him of a brief adventure she had had one day when she went up Hergest Ridge. Her enthusiastic eyes shone again in the reflected sunlight and the breeze blew strands of her blond hair over her face. She wiped them back with her bare sunburnt arm. Michael enjoyed looking at her and listening to her soft voice that was deeper than his sister's. His sister's voice was often too shrill.

Victoria began to tell him what had happened to her.

One day during the summer holidays of last year on a rain-swept morning she had been at home reading about the Ridge and some of the legends associated with it. She decided that she wanted to go up there on her own to explore the area and see if she could sense the atmosphere that the writer of the book maintained was still there, an atmosphere of the past and of latent mystery. So she persuaded her father to take her over there in the car when the weather was suitable. He agreed but insisted she take the dog with her. He didn't like her being up there on her own. He too, she thought, knew that there might be something uncanny at large on the Ridge. He therefore arranged a time to collect her when she would return from her expedition.

Everything was arranged; he took her mid-morning and dropped her off at the top of the hill just past Hergest Croft. She strode off up the hill, a rucksack on her back and the dog running out in front or her. She loved being up there, running, walking as the gentle cool breeze filled her with energy. Soon she had reached the highest point and sat down on a large stone to survey the land around her. She looked north to the Radnor Forest and then south towards the Brecon Beacons. She hummed and sang as she was truly elated by the atmosphere. She had expected a different atmosphere, one of sombre mystery, but she experienced a feeling of joy to be up there in the freedom of fresh air and distant views.

All of a sudden she was aware that her dog Nick was missing. She called out to him and walked further along the Ridge, thinking he might have strayed far ahead of her. She arrived at the edge of the Ridge at the yew tree where one can look down onto the village of Gladestry. He was nowhere to be seen. She ran back to the top of the Ridge, now in a slight panic. Perhaps Nick had fallen down a hole somewhere, or even worse had got among some sheep where an angry farmer would show him no mercy. She spent about an hour going backwards and forwards up there calling out his name. She met another walker with his dog, but he had not seen Nick.

She even went back to the beginning of the walk where her father had dropped her off. He was still nowhere to be seen. She started off back up the hill. She was now getting exhausted with all the worry and the vain effort. As she was approaching the group of stones where she some time ago had been sitting she saw what at first appeared to be a young man, then as she drew near an old man. Maybe she had at first been mistaken as she was slightly short-sighted. She drew nearer and saw that the old man, an elderly tramp he seemed, was carrying her dog. He then approached her holding the dog carefully in his arms.

He spoke to her: "Your dog managed to find his way down a hole and didn't want to come out. But I got hold of him and here he is."

He handed Nick to her. She thanked him, so relieved to have him back. The old tramp stood before her, his warm blue eyes and worn face seemed somehow reassuring that with him around the dog would not have got into any real danger. He asked her where she lived. She told him and then he replied:

"Your family live in these parts, and you will know how it is round here."

With these strange words he wished her farewell, turned and walked back to the stones. He disappeared behind the largest one. Victoria followed him a distance behind. When she reached the large stone he was nowhere to be seen. He had simply vanished as if into the ground, or even thin air! And as she looked at the stone it was for a moment a huge mirror in which she saw reflected her eyes and hair. Then the image was gone and the blank stone rested there unmoving embedded in the ground.

She looked at her watch and saw to her dismay that she was late and that her father would have been waiting for her for some time. She put Nick on his lead, turned and ran down the slope to where the car would be waiting. As she turned, though, she thought she heard soft singing from beneath the earth, but realized then it must be the wind which was now stronger than when she had commenced her expedition.

Her father was there, anxiously waiting for her. He had left the car and was striding up the hill calling out her name. She ran up to him and seized his arm.

"Nick went off and I couldn't find him for ages. Then an old tramp brought him to me. Nick had been stuck down a hole or something."

Her father was relieved at finding her but not altogether pleased at having to wait so long. He drove her back home silently, but, once at home told her the old tramp must have been Old Owen who was well known to those who lived in these parts.

"Old Jack who does odd jobs for Mr Pritchard can tell you a few things about him. He's quite harmless though, just a bit eccentric."

Victoria related all this to a fascinated Michael as the dog tugged at his lead.

"Just a short time to go before our exam results. Shall we celebrate or commiserate together?"

"Fine," he replied. "Let's hope we'll be happy on the day. My mother will phone my results through and I'll come round. By the way, I'm off with my uncle for a day or two near Rhayader."

"OK. Well, bye-bye for the moment, and enjoy yourselves. I'll see you when you get back."

She went off down the lane running with her dog that she had again let off the lead.

Michael turned back into the garden. He was in good spirits, happy that here was someone in his situation and such an attractive person into the bargain. He reflected too on the incident Victoria had related to him. She too had had an experience not exactly like his, but near enough just to hint at the mysteries that had so affected him. Maybe she knew more that she had told him today. Doubtless she was sensitive also to the atmosphere up there on Hergest Ridge. There may come a time, he mused, when he could share with her what he had been through.

The black birds still flew now and again over him, emerging from the scraggy clump of about one hundred yards away.

25

Before dinner he went on a short stroll with his uncle who needed fresh air and to stir up an appetite for the meal. He enjoyed the evening breeze and the chance to look out into distances after being cooped up in his study most of the afternoon.

On return he was more cheerful and stimulated by the thought of walking with his nephew in the hills trying to retrace old tracks and memories he had left there. The fears that had possessed him and held him back from returning had yielded to an enthusiasm and new-found energy born directly from what Michael had told him of his recent adventure.

They passed through the garden and were immediately alerted by loud barking. It was his enemies' dog that they had imprisoned in the shed. It was in a large pen covered with wire netting. Jack had been looking after it with scraps of food and attempting, often in vain, to clean the pen out from day to day. When it caught sight of Michael it bared its teeth.

"We can let it loose now," his uncle said. "I'll ask Jack to take it down the lane and let it find its own way home."

"But its owners have vanished. Shouldn't we hand it over to a dogs' home?

"All right then," he replied. "Jack can take it to a farm near Shobdon where they care for strays."

Uncle Hugh left Michael to rummage in the old lumber in the loft. He sorted out odds and ends that might be useful, pending what his uncle decided they needed for their camping: a small paraffin stove, a rucksack, a length of rope. He stumbled across an old hamper and went through its contents: he flicked through a couple of dusty books of the area and an old sketch book with drawings of houses in Presteigne, of the lane leading past the house, of the house itself and, very interesting, of two old men sitting together in what looked like the kitchen. There were a few old photographs of his uncle as he was many years ago with his brother and with his wife. Several copies of the last one were tucked into the back page of the album. He found one of his uncle in military uniform and an old sketch of Jack and Kate's cottage.. This one was framed and very old. There were old books and maps and a plan of a railway [never constructed] extending from Presteigne, taking it right through to Llangunllo where it was to join the line from Knighton. On one map Michael made out the old paths leading from the lane over the hills on either side, paths, maybe now overgrown from disuse or else ploughed up or made impassable by the planting of thorn hedges. There was a lightly drawn path by the Kings' Stones and a dotted line leading from Bach Hill past the Stones, up to Old Radnor church and turning to continue in the direction of Hergest Ridge. The Ridge itself would have been on an adjacent map.

He turned back to the pages of one of the old books and was reading about Radnorshire, *Sir Faesyfed* in Welsh – the 'drinking fields' – when his uncle shouted to him that supper was ready.

He came down the ladder and, looking out of the landing window, noticed that Jack had already taken the dog away, and in the twilit trees at the garden's end were perching two birds, those two birds, he guessed, that had flown over him this afternoon, and that had cast their shadows, momentarily darkening Victoria's eyes.

He saw them as some sort of a threat. They flew up from the trees with loud cawing, high over the edge of the horizon into the light of the summer evening to vanish eastwards over the roof of a barn and the cottage. Michael, grabbing the binoculars, rushed outside to look at them more closely, but they were gone, and in any case it was time to join his uncle at table.

Uncle Hugh looked agitated; he was nervous about the coming expedition, whilst at the same time looking forward with some excitement to being away for a short period. Michael asked him about the old books and papers he had found in the loft, and he was invited to bring them down after supper to look at them at leisure. He asked more about the history of this area.

"I have told you all I can, I think. It was near here that the first written mention was made of Parsifal or Perceval, the knight of the Holy Grail, the one pure knight who had found the Grail castle again after it had been lost all those centuries."

He told Michael of Joseph of Arimithea arriving in Britain with the sacred chalice wherein Christ's shed blood had been caught as He was dying on the Cross, the Sacred Blood that had brought redemption to the world and was now the eternal promise of salvation for all men. When harder times had come, and enemies of the Grail appeared, the sacred brotherhood had been forced to hide till a better time arrived when all might once more accept and enjoy these mysteries. Uncle Hugh talked as if he half believed all this or at least that there was something in the legend. Such a company might still exist, preserving and perpetuating their secrets till ... He paused and smiled as though he was playing on his nephew's active imagination and wished to entertain him. He really had graver matters on his mind, but Michael pieced all this together with his journey into the world below the world, where that hidden company had shown itself to him.

"There is a dimension somewhere, I feel it very near us here," his uncle's kind voice continued," that goes beyond what you and I sense in our everyday lives. For some just one minute in their life gives them a glimpse of it; they do not even notice it, perhaps. Others are blessed with longer, cherish it, try to keep it for ever."

Michael could not add to what he said. He saw that his uncle was visibly moved as he continued:

"Hanging on to whatever wonderful things you have experienced is not enough. It can be a seed. If planted it must grow, expand and take you to a broader, higher level of existence. And one day, who knows how, it can return if we still have the will and are prepared to accept the way it chooses to reappear."

Then he added gravely:

"Of course, hanging on to the past can destroy as well."

He stood up and fetched a half-full bottle of wine from the cabinet.

"This is ours, Michael. Let us drink to a happy time in the hills."

Michael's mind was flitting from one subject to another; so much had he heard to stimulate him. He shot from a vision of that hall and the company beneath the Ridge to their forthcoming adventure in the mountains, and then to his uncle's task and to his encounter with Victoria that day. He asked whether his uncle had seen those two crows circling the locality. Did he think there was something sinister about them?

His uncle said little, but Michael sensed that he knew Michael had been mixed up in something he did not understand and might possibly find threatening. He was not entirely at ease. He felt they must be careful where they went and where they put things they might need. A marauder might be about. After all, that dog had been sent here and Michael had been kidnapped, and the culprits were missing.

"Look at the evening light," he remarked to Michael, pointing through the window. The evening was calm, the sky clear save for clusters of insects moving from one place to another. But there were strange colours in the air, now tinting what they could see of the horizon through the trees at the end of the garden. The fading light spread in an almost imperceptible sheen over parts of the garden.

"There is no birdsong this evening," he muttered. "The birds are silent or have been chased away. And those colours, where do they come from? Inside us? Or are we witnessing something outside, a change in things, a sign of danger maybe?"

Michael imagined what up to now he had only read about; a sort of struggle between forces, one alien, a struggle in which he had become involved.

"If there is a danger here, then there is something of value too, lurking around, seeking to break forth and show itself. Where danger is redeeming powers grow too. Who wrote that? Do you know?"

Michael did not. He suggested they bolt the doors and lock everything up that night and retire early to bed. This they did, and the sky on this day, which had enjoyed bright sunlight, was light till late, with wisps of green and red, and at times a faint shadow of moonlit blue from an enormous tree.

26

The warm air and sun on his face all day, the burning on his face after he had withdrawn from the sunlight – these factors lulled Michael into another deep sleep that night.

As he drifted off he led himself as if now by instinct through the countryside around the house, over fields and hills, past groups of trees and stones to Hergest Ridge, deep down where he had seen, eyes like living jewels, the central part of a person, as a lake central to landscape reflects and expresses it and the sky it lies under, if one gazes in deep and long enough. The face and flowing hair lulled him into sleep. Thus he slept dreaming and half awake till the light of early morning touched him. He closed his eyes, but the images had fled. Where to? And where had they come from?

He had pulled himself half-heartedly out of bed before he remembered that tomorrow he was off with his uncle into the mountains beyond Rhayader, and that today they had to go into Presteigne to make a few purchases before setting off. He had to rouse himself from the breakfast table out to the car which his uncle had taken out onto the drive and started up. They drove at a leisurely pace along the quiet country lanes into the small town. It was hot and fairly sultry, and Michael therefore found it pleasant to stroll down to the old bridge over the river Lugg while his uncle bought what was necessary. The rippling of the clear soft water held him for a while as he leaned over the stone wall of the bridge, watching the reflections of the passing clouds on the surface of the water. Small twigs and fallen petals and leaves were carried downstream. Then he drew himself up from his leaning position and sauntered back into town.

Here it was so quiet in contrast to the bustle in his hometown. It was an old country town of mainly half-timbered houses on the two principal streets.

He met his uncle as arranged under the eaves of the broad white house in the main street. He was given a large bag of provisions to carry.

"Better than getting them in Rhayader; we don't want any delays when we are there. I'll just fill up with petrol and then we can go home."

They stacked what had been bought into the boot of the car, climbed in, drove to a petrol station and within twenty minutes were back home. They left their purchases in the car and started to load other necessities in. Michael was becoming increasingly excited when he thought of the vastness of the territory they were about to visit. He had studied the ordnance survey map of that area, had spread the map out in front of him and seen the huge region of roadless uninhabited landscape where they were going to walk. There seemed to be few footpaths in an area of hills, U and V-shaped valleys and countless streams and waterfalls. His spirit rose at their coming enterprise.

He begged his uncle to lend him his bicycle that afternoon, and after lunch he sailed down the lane in the heavy air to have another look at the Kings' Stones before they left next morning.

"Be quick," Uncle Hugh said. "I can feel a storm brewing."

Michael pedalled as hard as he could in the sultry heat, down all the lanes which were now so familiar to him. He reached the Stones a little breathless and rested for a while under a fragrant hedge. Then he rose to his feet and, somewhat apprehensive, went up to the Stones. He walked round them, viewing them from all angles, how this one tilted this way and that one the other. He noted the slant of the tallest of the four, all outlined in their own pattern against the hills around them as he stooped to make them seem high monoliths.

He sought the hole where he had once hidden the staff. Where was the piece of turf that he had pulled up? He found it at the foot of a stone. It had already started to grow back into the soil again. All the same he managed to yank it up. The small gap was still there, and a narrow hole going into the earth. He lay down to look in further. Down it went into the earth, dark so that he saw nothing save the side of the enormous granite stone. Maybe, though, he heard very distantly voices: they might have been singing as before, but not the old mournful song. It was surely a song of rejoicing, revitalized, faster, more strongly accented and more freely sung than before. Perhaps then the company was down there, renewed by the return of the staff that was their spear.

The sound of thunder brought him abruptly to his feet. His uncle had warned him of an impending storm and now it was approaching. He must get back before it broke.

He replaced the turf, mounted the bike and went as fast as he could back along the lanes he had come.

He was riding down the lane to his uncle's house when the first drops fell and was scarcely inside when the heavy rain started. During dinner the storm subsided, and Michael was sure it had passed. His uncle contradicted him: it had passed over but would soon return. The air was still heavy and needed to empty itself of its weight.

They went to bed at a good hour to be able to start early the next morning. Michael lay in bed staring at the dull shadows the light was casting on the ceiling, going over all that had happened to him since he had come to this house, thinking how all he had experienced had changed him since he had left home, and how he, for the first time, had witnessed something he knew to be beautiful, how he had gone down that narrow passageway, through the gate to the root of the world. He knew too how warm his affection had become for his wonderful uncle. He was so grateful to be treated as a young man and not as a child or even a teenager.

He fell asleep. At the end of the night, just before daybreak the violent thunder returned, and the curtains of rain shut off the house from the landscape in sheets of thrown-down water. He awoke, went over to the window and watched it all happening. He stood for some time at the window. Then overcome by tiredness and the sudden drop in temperature, he went back to bed and slept till he was awakened with the dampening words:

"We'll have a job getting down the lane for a while; it's flooded quite deep."

Michael staggered to his feet and looked out of the window at the water swirling down the lane; the stream had overflowed, despite the ditches that had been dug in the spring. The water would need to subside by several inches before the car could get safely through it.

After breakfast he packed his night things and whatever else he thought he might require. He found the rope that he had stupidly forgotten lying at the bottom of a drawer. He had concealed it under some newspaper.

"And I promised to destroy it," he muttered, ashamed.

He packed it, intending to throw it into some chasm they might walk past when they were in the mountains. But he had a premonition that they might somehow need it at a given time. There might still be some threat hanging over him, a danger that he would have to deal with.

The floods subsided faster than they had reckoned, for Jack had managed to channel off the water into a field. They wished the old couple goodbye and drove off down the lane, waving to Victoria as they passed her. She was out in her wellingtons walking her frisky dog. She waved after them as they drove out of the area and, after some twenty minutes, through Bleddfa and Penybont, eventually to Rhayader where his uncle acquired from a local shopkeeper the key to the old cottage in the mountains. They drove on and turned right, as he had said they would, under the railway bridge and were soon climbing the old coach road high into the mountains, much higher than Hergest Ridge.

Down below them to their left was an isolated lake. High above the lake so that they cast no shadow, the crows hovered in the lighter air as they prepared to descend.

27

The half-dead hawthorns, through which they saw the lake [for it was at this point that they stopped to allow the engine to cool before the ascent] cut their own shapes, clawed themselves out of the lake, as though with the talons of the birds of prey that perched in them. The rope that Michael carried in his back trouser pocket was burning hard against him, reminding him to get rid of it, as the brave rider had bidden him.

But he was still holding on to it, nursing a secret fear that up here his trials might well continue, and he would need this last link he had with that hidden world. And as the rope burnt its presence against him, the crows were there, perched in the tree, staring at them, larger than what he took to be normal crows. They stopped to survey the mountain scene. Michael saw through the binoculars their eyes. They were uncannily like those of his enemies who had taken him and dragged him under. He had thought them vanquished, but could they be still present in another form? Yes, he was sure. He was still their prey: in their transformation into these shadow birds, lustreless enemies of the sunlight, they sat and awaited their opportunity to destroy what they could of the world below. Their sharp beaks could peck out his eyes.

Michael and his uncle looked up at the trees. The branches, half dead from fungus growth, held those henchmen, watching, waiting. The birds themselves were malignant fungus on a pure blue sky.

"This place is haunted," Michael murmured. "Shall we move on?"

His uncle nodded, and the car started on the steep climb to the summit of the pass. Here at the top was a breeze and the rush of water tumbling down the valley, an area freer, open to rapid changes of air. The car slowed down at this point and his uncle guided it onto a wide verge.

"We can leave it here and unload. The old shepherd's cottage is over there, about a mile, if I remember, tucked into a hollow."

They secured the car, placing rocks under the wheels and then took the two large rucksacks from the boot. His uncle took a stout walking stick, locked the car and they set off down the rough track into the wilderness – no trees except an odd one bravely alive in a small cranny by a large cast-down rock that shielded it from the wind – no other vegetation but grass, hard clumps of it that they had to tread their way through, and the dry rocks, solitary or in small clusters, and a view that expanded for miles over the barren upland.

After an hour's walking they came to the old building. It was further over to the west than his uncle had reckoned, and sunk down in a hollow, sheltered from the prevailing wind by an outcrop of rock, an ancient dolmen, perhaps.

Uncle Hugh produced a long key, turned with difficulty and pushed the door open. It was not quite as he remembered it: the walls had been repaired, reinforced, and part of the soil floor had been overlaid by a low wooden platform on which they could sleep. But the old fire-grate was still there and the hob on which to boil the water and to cook. They laid their packs down and Michael stepped outside, followed by his uncle, to view the land about them. To the west the hills seemed to stretch into infinity, but after a while they made out on the horizon the same coloured glow they had seen at home in Radnorshire and the hint of an enormous forest ranging from one side to the other.

"Let's have something to eat and then get to sleep; we can then start out early in the morning," Uncle Hugh suggested. Michael concurred. He knew or half-knew what this small expedition meant to his uncle. It was an attempt, Michael thought, to recover what he could of the past when he had been happier.

They found sticks and one or two logs lying in one corner, enough indeed to cook by.

They sat outside while the meal cooked to avoid the oppressive heat of the fire. Uncle Hugh showed him on the map where he had walked with his wife and where he planned they should make for during the time at their disposal. Now and then Michael looked up anxiously to the sky. It had taken on the opulent blue of the evening, but there were no birds in the air, nothing at all flying in the sky.

They slept well that night although the floor was hard. They were to get up at sunrise, though Michael was unconscious of this as he slept through his dreams of songs, sad and happy, dreams of dark, long endless passages and a vast open hall thronged with fine-clad people. Then he was out in the wind and rain on a journey, forever onward, till the halls of treeland enclosed him and never seemed to let him go. The trees' leaves fell in the soon-to-come autumn and blew round his feet: they called to his mind huge black birds that would peck at him as the winter frost set in.

He woke up, frightened, seizing the rope from his trouser pocket and then clutching it the rest of the night.

His uncle was shaking him by the shoulders.

"Wake up! Wake up! We shall have to move off soon."

He had already kindled a fire and the water was murmuring in the pot. Michael obeyed, dazed and still half in his dream world. They breakfasted inside and packed what they would be needing. Michael volunteered to carry the tent for the first stretch.

They helped each other on with their packs and prepared to set off, map in hand. His uncle took the spade which was leaning against an outside wall and dowsed the fire. He stood the spade against the wall again, came out and locked the door. They both watched the clouds of smoke rising from the chimney as the fire went out, clouds rising into the air, covering the roof of the cottage, billowing over to the solitary twisted tree and its gnarled branches. In the tree, as he and his uncle looked, those crows again were watching them. They flapped their wings slowly, rising into the air through the dispersing smoke. They were over them beating their wings and furiously cawing.

They looked up and beheld not two birds but a mass of winged blackness moving down on them, shifting the heavy air – as thunder from near at hand deafened their ears. The black crows with their taloned feet were grabbing out beneath them, clawing like old thorn branches for prey. Further they descended beating the air in fury.

Michael and his uncle shied back and away, but the black bird-cloud fell even closer. The very weight of feathers was stuffing the fresh air out and the light. They were breathing suffocating feather-down and saw less and less. Led by the two great birds that had been shadowing them they alighted on their shoulders and heads to peck at their cheeks and were reaching for their eyes and ears.

"Get back into the cottage!" yelled his uncle, rummaging in his pocket for the key, for he had to defend his eyes. Michael threw himself to the ground, his hands round his head in an attempt to ward off the attack. But their claws were fastening into his back and neck, drawing blood. His hand searched for his pocket, found the rope and tried to beat the birds off with it. Some shied back higher into the air with wild piercing squawks, but the two leaders flew over and with their long crooked beaks seized the rope.

Michael heard himself crying out: "Burn the rope! Set it alight! Fire it! Fire it!"

His uncle shot over to him, as if Michael's pleas had thrown an idea into him. He took a lighter from his pocket and flicked it on. A flame rose. Again some birds shied away, but others drove in closely and persistently.

"Light the rope!" Michael screamed, as the two large birds descended on him. Michael flung himself at them, ignoring the other birds that clung to his hair and clothes. He grabbed one end of the rope and held it to the flame that his uncle had kindled.

Immediately a huge flash hurled them to the ground and flung itself through the entire sky around them. There was a terrified shriek, the mad flutter of wings and a bright light of flame shot up to them, setting fire to them and quenching the darkness that the wings had brought. For a time uncle and nephew dared not look into the sky.

They remained for a while there on the ground, kneeling, gazing at the rough earth, till their eyes were ready for the sky again. They both raised their heads as the morning sun beat down on the back of their necks, drying, healing their wounds. In front of them, to the west a huge sheet of flame was receding, burning nothing, destroying nothing, transforming, taking the old landscape they had observed and seen as real, and recreating it; for them it was a new landscape. Michael looked at his uncle who was gazing out in front of them to the path that he clearly intended them to take. It was as if, in the eyes of Hugh Pritchard, the landscape he had trodden in those past days was coming again to life in him, as though those rich days when he had walked it with Alice were at least partly returning, giving him the strength he needed to stride out and discover what he had come here to find.

They were standing up again, making certain the packs were secure on their backs as they paced forward to take the path that led out in front of them.

28

With their feet they had pushed the scattered dead feathers aside as they made their way along the path, up a gentle slope then down a little, joining a stream that had just emerged from the ground. A slight breeze blew through their hair as the land opened before them.

"This is a drovers' road," said his uncle. " It is designated as 'ancient path' on the ordnance survey map."

They were descending slowly into a broad valley. On either side of the path rocks stood at irregular intervals. From time to time they passed an odd clump of old trees clinging to the hard ground for there was little deep soil in which they could thrive.

"This is the way, I remember," his uncle indicated as the path appeared to fork, and they took the less obvious path over a hillock and down a steeper slope where were to their left the remains of what must have been a shepherd's summer cottage.

"It's strange," he added, "if I had tried at home to tell you which way I couldn't have done so, but now with the landscape before me my memories start to come back. It was just beyond here, I recall that we stopped for a break. It was hot and Alice was feeling a little tired. We must have spent an hour or so here for we had plenty of time; it was the very beginning of September and the days were still fairly long. I think I nodded off too, because I was awakened by her touch and felt her holding my hand. She kissed me and then ..."

He ceased talking and Michael could see tears in his eyes.

"But we shan't stop," he said firmly. "We must get on."

They heard the sound of birds again. Above them flew white-crested birds, scattering the light as it flashed reflected off their bodies when their wings spread, and they floated from high up down above the uncle and his nephew as if showing them the way.

They walked for two hours or so till the heat made them thirsty and foot-weary. They rested at the side of a rapid stream, dipping their feet and drinking the clear pure water.

"How much further?" Michael asked.

His uncle was not sure. As he reminded Michael, he and Alice had had to turn back. They had never completed their planned walk. He reckoned though that they had quite a way to go still and would need to get a move on to be sure of reaching their goal.

"This has once more become so familiar, though the path we need to take will not be familiar."

Uncle Hugh sat very still. He was not looking towards where his eyes appeared to be looking, but onto an invisible screen stretched out before him, and through this screen to a world that he and his dead wife had come so near to finding. Now he was close again after all these years, and after all the hard work he had put in at home in his attempt to record those happy days in the past. Whether it was too much for him or whether he was doing the right thing preyed on him. Perhaps this was the only way he could find out. From the vast store in his mind he was groping back for the remnants that might come within his grasp, so that he could assemble them and make sense of a past that haunted him with its fragments.

They trudged on. The ground was rougher now as he had predicted, and he warned Michael to take care lest he sprain an ankle. At length they reached a hollow where the ground was flatter, more even, and close to a stream.

"We should settle here for the night," his uncle directed and asked Michael to help him select the best spot for the tent. They found a place, slightly higher and level, a green bank, soft enough to drive the pegs in. A couple of trees provided shade and kept the wind off the fire they kindled to cook their meal. The white-crested birds perched on the rocks a short distance away and seemed to be watching over them as they ate and prepared their sleeping bags. The sun went down behind the hill to the northwest.

"I feel no threat from those birds at all," Michael remarked. The campfire crackled with the dry sticks and bits of branch they had put on it. It lit up in spasms the near landscape. They spoke little to each other and soon retired to sleep until dawn.

At dawn they awoke and were pleased that the fine dry weather continued. They ate a frugal breakfast, cleared the tent from the ground, gathered up their things and set off again in the direction they had been walking yesterday. Ahead of them were the remains of an old oak forest. The friendly birds flew ahead of them and settled on the branches. The path led under the trees, and they looked up at the filtered light that the pale leaves let through. The birds looked down onto them and flew then ahead leading the way again, but disappeared as Michael and his uncle walked further in the wood. They were replaced by smaller birds that flitted chirping restlessly, but always keeping up with the two walkers.

They now began to climb up a much steeper slope.

"This is where we gave up." His uncle halted, looked back along the path they had come and seemed to be quite lost in deep thought. He whirled his stick absent-mindedly round and round. The expression on his face changed. Michael stood silent at his side. He knew this might be the moment. He watched his uncle's expression as his brow wrinkled and then his face relaxed again.

He said with a note of desperation: "I don't know why. Why, why did we not go on? We had the time and were quite fresh."

Michael, out of sympathy, took his uncle's hand. At once his uncle responded. Michael had awoken something asleep within him.

"That's it," he exclaimed. "We'd met just here in this spot an old shepherd who told us the war had started, and Alice knew she had to get back at once to London. Those were her orders. You see she was needed immediately, as she was in some special group in the War Ministry. And I was straightaway called up into the army. How stupid of me that I should have forgotten! Thank you Michael. Touching me brought back the answer. It was here in this spot that she took hold of my hand and apologized for spoiling our trip. And then, of course the war came, the bombers, the Blitz and I never saw her again."

Michael did not look at him; he did not wish to see his uncle weeping.

At length his uncle mopped his brow and eyes, patted his nephew on the shoulder, and they set off again along the path Hugh had not taken with his wife.

29

They gazed down into a valley. The path was wilder now and less obvious; it led on irregular ground up between rocks and down again over swampy ground, through reeds and over small areas of marsh. They had once or twice to find or create stepping stones over a brook, on one occasion they took their boots off to paddle over a fast-flowing stream. At the valley's end they made out the ruined abbey. They trudged down towards it.

The white birds appeared, flying ahead of them as a westerly breeze carried to them a whiff of sea air.

It was as his uncle had predicted: within half an hour or little more they reached the ruins. Only parts of the walls of the refectory still stood, yet the outline of the Abbey church was discernible over to the right and next to it the graveyard with its sunken stones where the monks had lain for centuries.

A strange atmosphere prevailed here, as if they had reached a land beyond. Hugh paused while he thought of what he wished to say. He took Michael by the arm and spoke:

"You know this gives me an idea, a little something I could write, a short story perhaps, an attempt to uncover a thing or two I might have forgotten. I imagine arriving here after a long journey, not knowing what was in store, and finding a charm or secret that could bring this community back to life. The walls would rise, the chapel stand rebuilt and the monks or friars all assemble for daily prayers. They had been exiled all these years beneath the soil, waiting for somebody to bring them back. It's fantasy, I know, but maybe you understand what I am trying to get at. It might be better than attempting to rehash a diary."

Michael hesitated to reply; his uncle was striking a note in him. Was he, in a roundabout way, hinting that he knew about his nephew's recent adventure? No, that was unlikely.

After a few moments he answered:

"I like it. I think I know what you mean. There are things of value absent from us now, but which may return should we find a way."

He was proud of this utterance.

Hugh was, it seemed, alone again in his thoughts.

"You know, Michael, when a person dear to you has died, you think first of things you wish you had said to her, or him, and what you might have done together. That's what you find out when you have lost her, and it is painful indeed."

Michael turned away unwilling to see the expression on his uncle's face. They took a last glance at the ruins and Hugh suggested they go back.

"We have little time. We shall be better off at home," were Hugh's quiet words.

Thus his uncle walked, head down, upwards to the hills, whence they had come and where he and Alice had once turned back. They had almost reached the top when he flopped down on the grass next to a boulder. His energy was momentarily sapped. Michael turned to survey the distance they had already covered and sat down next to him.

"It's no good, Michael. I'm scarcely up to the task. It is foolish to expect to uncover what I had failed to find when I was younger. I've been treating time as if it were space, just a stretch of land I might walk back across. That's nonsense; I can't step back."

Hugh wiped his brow. "We'll walk straight back to the cottage now. No further night in the tent. I've had enough."

By mid-evening they reached the old cottage. Michael took charge of things as his uncle was too tired. He took the provisions they had and made a meal as best he could. His mind was wandering from the golden hall beneath the earth, where he had first seen those eyes, to the landscape above.

He made up the fire once more before he too lay down to rest. Between his reveries he looked at his uncle: his face showed the strain of these days and his breathing was irregular.

Outside a wind was getting up. As Hugh's breathing grew louder, so the storm rose as though to break above it. Then there was a lull in the wind and the air grew hot, beating in on them with a heat greater that that of the fire. It was stifling hot. Michael had to open a shutter to let fresh air in, but, of course, the air outside was not cooler. He could not bear to lie down in this temperature. He took the remainder of the water in the pot and threw it on the fire. In vain; the steam rose in profusion, too great to escape up the chimney. It spread inside the cottage; he could no longer make out his uncle asleep on the wooden platform.

There was one enormous clap of thunder; he opened the door; outside the rain was falling in sheets and pounding like acorns falling on the corrugated iron roof. The air started to cool. He could see his uncle; his breathing was now more regular; he seemed to have come through the worst. Michael knew now he could sleep peacefully.

The morning came with fresh sunlight and the promise of a calmer day. He managed to kindle a fire and prepare warm drinks. They packed their things and set off for the car. Michael carried both packs for the short distance. Hugh was grateful for he was still weary. He panted behind Michael in the moistened air.

A short distance from the cottage they both turned to look back at where they had been; it was the highest point in their walk. They looked back at the cottage, crouched in its hollow, shielded supposedly from the elements. They looked further: the path they had taken moved out westwards. That was the land they were leaving behind.

"Look," said Michael. "They have started to plant a new forest."

It was so: far into the distance stretched patterns of straight lined ditches holding their saplings. The landscape they had known was changing into a landscape they would not know.

They reached the car, dropped the packs into the boot and drove off. Hugh returned the key to the shop where he had borrowed it.

30

His uncle drove slowly back, and they stopped several times, at various cafés and pubs en route, to refresh themselves. Hugh Pritchard was tired. His face looked drained; Michael was concerned when once they swerved into the side of the road, only to correct the error in the nick of time. On the way Hugh telephoned Kate to tell her when to expect them, asking her to prepare a good meal, for Michael was very hungry.

They arrived back safely and Michael was relieved; he knew how much their adventure had taken it out of his uncle. He returned downstairs, having changed his clothes. Hugh looked bad. His face was worn; his eyes just slits.

"He's extremely tired as you can see," Michael remarked to Kate. "Our trip took a lot out of him, but I think he's happier for it."

Hugh had a bite to eat and retired early to bed. He remained in bed in the morning, requesting not to be disturbed. It was therefore annoying when the telephone rang loudly at about half past eleven. Kate rushed to lift the receiver before it disturbed his uncle. It was Michael's mother.

"What on earth does she want," he asked as if she were someone of little importance, interfering. The holiday had made his life at home seem mundane and so far away in every sense. He was being rudely shaken out of a wonderful dream.

"Come quickly. It's important," Kate whispered to him.

And it was important; his mother had his exam results; they were good, good enough for acceptance on the university course he had chosen, even though one grade was disappointing. His sister had not done so well in her exams. She was upset. Michael rejoiced that he was not at home. He told Kate of his success and was congratulated, but cautioned to wait till his uncle came down to tell him. He would be delighted to hear the results when he was ready.

Michael, however, was more interested in informing somebody else. He wanted to go across to Victoria's, tell her his news and find out how she had done. He hoped she would be her cheerful self and have good news for him. He went out quickly by the back garden and strode down the path behind her house. She was coming out towards him.

"Guess what!" she cried out half dancing and waving in the air the paper with her results. "I've got all I wanted including two top grades. How have you done?"

"All right," he replied. "Well done. You have done well, and I've got my university place. I expect you have too."

There was no trace in him of envy that she had maybe done better than him; he was glad for her and that was that.

"Yes, I'm OK too. What a relief." She stood there in front of him, smiling blissfully and communicating her warmth as her eyes seemed to dance in the sunlight.

"And do you know what? My mum and dad want you and your uncle to come to dinner this evening. We must celebrate. Say you'll accept!"

They went back into her house for coffee and sat together in the kitchen chatting about their futures and what plans they had. There was a lot to settle: finance, grants, confirmation of a place and so on. But they had the assurance they had worked and hoped for.

Michael returned just in time for lunch. He was relieved to find his uncle sitting at the head of the table looking better. He got up at once, came up to his nephew and took him by the hand.

"Well done, well done," he said. "Your success makes me very happy."

After lunch he called him into his study. He was seated in his familiar position, in his swivel chair, pipe in mouth with his large diary before him.

"I should like to thank you for coming with me on the expedition. Without you it would not have been a success. I would still be brooding here on the answer to my question. I wish to ask you one thing though: when I am gone will you take my diary, add what I have been unable to add and keep it carefully, copy it if you can so that it is more secure from loss. I want to know that this part of me will survive and memory of Alice with it. Will you do that? Look after it carefully when the time comes."

Michael found words inadequate. He hugged his uncle, moved that so much should be entrusted to him.

"Of course I promise," he answered eventually, knowing that the diary would preserve indirectly memories of this wonderful holiday when he had experienced more than he could ever have imagined, and indeed discovered another world that complemented his own.

"Please let me say, Uncle," he began, "marrying Alice was the best thing you ever did. Perhaps the short time you were together has given you the strength to go on."

Hugh was moved by these words. He turned away, looked out of the study window at the chestnut trees whose leaves were already turning brown for autumn.

He replied: "You're right son. I should have realized that long ago. It is wonderful though to hear such wisdom coming from a young man."

He changed his tone. "Now about this evening: Victoria's father was round this morning and has kindly invited both of us to dinner. Of course, we'll both go. I look forward to it. They expect us about seven. Now I must ask you to leave me; I need a rest."

Michael went out once more, hoping to catch Victoria taking her dog out, but she was not to be seen. Maybe she was helping her mother to prepare for the evening. He leapt over a stile a hundred yards down the lane and walked up towards the ruins of Stapleton Castle. He was in a way glad after all to be alone, for he had time to think back on how his life had changed since he had been here: how narrow his world had been a month ago! It had broadened, starting with him questioning his father about the staff, the encounter with the old tramp in the field behind their house and then, on arriving here, everything had, as it were, accelerated, and he had become involved in an adventure he could never have dreamed of, culminating in that vision in the underground hall and the revelation of the world beyond his world. Was it, he asked himself, as real as the reality of his exam results? He was uncertain, for his adventure seemed even more real. His home and academic success were for the moment more remote. Time would tell, maybe. But his success brought him closer to Victoria who, with his uncle, was inextricably bound up in his life here. She was not entirely uninvolved in his adventures. It was pretty clear that she too had encountered Old Owen, and that was not the only way she was involved.

He wondered one day if he would be able to see a pattern to everything or whether life would always be confusing. He thought of his uncle and how long it was taking him to piece together his life. He had, out of sympathy, taken hold of his hand as they had stood together in the mountains. He wondered if a seemingly unimportant gesture like that, might, in the future, enlighten him.

He did not venture far that afternoon. He went back, read for a while and chatted to Kate. He was awaiting the evening.

31

His uncle was up and about again at six o'clock. He looked well rested and was dressed more smartly than usual. Michael too put on what smart clothes he had brought with him. They set out just before seven to walk the two hundred yards to Victoria's house. Her parents greeted and congratulated Michael on his success.

Victoria immediately asked Michael if he would care to see their garden. She took him by the arm, and they strolled around the garden together, chatting about their immediate future. She wanted to know when he was going home.

"No need to rush back for school now," she smiled at him. He agreed and was sure his uncle would not mind if he prolonged his stay a little.

She showed him the footpath which crossed the back of their garden and which led eventually up onto the hill past the ruins of Stapleton Castle, where, she said, the views were marvellous. She took him by the hand and led him a short way up the path until they heard the voices of others who had come out after them, calling them in to dinner. It was a merry meal with plenty of lively conversation that lasted till well after nine o'clock. He was asked about what he had been doing during his time here. He answered, saying as much as he wished to divulge. He should have said more; he knew the family might possibly have accepted an account of his adventure had he told it in modified form. Nevertheless he kept it to himself. In fact it seemed strangely in the past after the expedition with his uncle and now his new friend here. The happy evening took his mind off other things, even off his exam success.

Victoria took him to her father's study to show him books on the area that she knew interested him as they had always interested her since she had learned to appreciate the beautiful countryside and landscape in these parts. Her attractive blue eyes flashed back at him as he tentatively halted outside the study door. As she turned, her long blond hair brushed lightly against his cheek.

"It's all right," she assured him. "My father doesn't mind us browsing in his room. He's glad that I show interest."

Michael followed. She showed him a couple of books on legends of the area and a book of Welsh legends that dealt with areas further west. There were books on the local wild flowers and woodland, but most of all he wanted to see the maps, especially one of the old ones made at the end of the nineteenth century. But she was keener on showing him a more detailed recent map of this area. She opened the map, her shoulder touching his as she did so.

"Look. Here's a path going up hill from your uncle's house. The view from the top of the hill is fabulous especially when the sun rises."

She looked at him, maybe a little shyly:

"Shall I call for you tomorrow morning about an hour before sunrise? That will be about five o'clock. We can walk up there. I can show you how lovely it is."

"I'd like that very much," Michael replied immediately. "I shall be up, don't worry."

They returned to the others in the lounge where all were drinking coffee.

Soon it was time to go and to thank the family for their hospitality. Michael was particularly warm in his thanks, for he could scarcely recall an evening that he had enjoyed so much.

He slept in fits and starts. He was worried lest he should oversleep and not be ready when she arrived. However, there was no danger of that. He was up at half past four, washed, snatched a piece of bread and drank a glass of fruit juice. He stood outside waiting for her. It was chilly, and he wore his light anorak.

At five almost on the dot she came walking briskly up the lane, smiling at him as he went to the gate to meet her.

"Hi, good morning," she greeted him. "Here, we take this stile," and they both bounded over and set off at a pace along the winding path and up the hill.

After a time they reached a narrow lane lined with hedgerows on either side. They passed Stapleton Castle and began the steep climb up the lane.

"This is the way up to the Kite's nest. Oh, it's only the name of a house up there and down a track. That is where the beautiful view is."

They strode up the steep incline, stopping only a moment to take in breath and to peer through a field gap to see how high they had already climbed. Eventually they were at the top and the sun was still not up.

"We go along here," she said pointing down a wide path signed to the Kite's nest. At a point where they could see out over the landscape she stopped.

"Here is the best view," Victoria said. Michael looked over the fields and hillocks to the horizon where the light of the sun was glowing more and more brightly.

"How lovely everything looks," he whispered softly as he stood close to her.

"Wait a minute," she said, "while I put on my glasses."

The sun was now just peeping over the distant horizon, filling every living thing with its warm gold light.

"There," she murmured softly," Now I can see everything clearly."

She slipped her hand gently into his. Their eyes fanned out over the countryside before them – the browned fields, some already harvested, the hedgerows creating their various patterns, the trees dotted and clumped and above all the birds singing, soaring and diving and carving their lines over the morning mists.

Michael held her hand firmly and turned to look at her. Her lovely radiant eyes shone into his, her glasses reflecting the rays of the sun.

The dawn came on with its increasing light, dispersing the mists and streaming warmth into their young bodies and so much more. Here summed up in this moment was all Michael had experienced in his wonderful days out here.

Suddenly their peace was rudely interrupted: a screaming jet fighter shot over the landscape. She clutched his hand more tightly as he pulled her to him.

"I hope there's not going to be another war," she whispered.

"I hope that too," he replied. "I like things just as they are."

THE END